# The Seed
## (ORIGIN OF AI)

by
Amurá Oñaā

Published by

UNLIMITED LLC
2018

This material is a work of fiction. All of the characters and names are products of the author's imagination or used fictitiously.

ISBN 978-0-692-14454-1
THE SEED (ORIGIN OF AI)

Cover Design and Art by Amurá Oñaā

Published by Amurá Unlimited LLC

www.amuraunlimited.com

To the Dreamers

# 1

How long had it been? Did it matter? Questions, swirling like the wind, blew in from every direction, at awkward angles, slicing downward out from nowhere, breaking upward from the mountain below; they squeezed her like a vice tightening on every side. They came in recklessly, without warning, allowing little to no time for answers or clarity, leaving no room for a reasonable response. They slashed at her like the savage icy wind howling around her, keeping her pressed against the mountainside.

Dr. Yohanna Eleazar, seizing a chance to regain control of herself and her situation, only to lose it, began to question everything, from her sanity to decisions made more than four weeks ago to help her "companions" escape civilization. There was little room to think, only quick, brief moments where a thought or two could stand on their own for a few seconds before being shattered. So she struggled to use what slimmer of the time she had available to her to adjust the instrument settings on her left sleeve in an attempt to reconfigure the calibrations that her advanced thermal enhancement gear needed to keep it from malfunctioning. She must have damaged her suit the day before when she lost her footing and slid twenty meters or more down one of the mountain's slopes. Her team was able to pull her back to safety, but something in her suit was amiss. It had been at least two days on this

God-forsaken trail alongside the Himalayan mountain range, and the sky was growing darker. The decision to climb made sense a day or two ago. However, now it was beyond her, even though the trust in her team was there. The pain she was dealing with created its own set of doubts about her also being here.

They walked ahead of her with one behind, watching her back, seemingly purely determined or merely unaffected by the cold wind that whirled around them. But then, of course, all five of them were Platinum Tier 97 Androids, the most advanced AI robots known to man. A unique monumental achievement, in and of itself, and a byproduct of Dr. Eleazar's genius; an enhancement in robotic engineering that had leapfrogged the whole AI international program decades ahead, changing, if not rewriting, history itself.

"Doctor, I can detect your life signs, and the problem with your thermal outfit is exacerbating your condition," said one of them, who walked back over to her. She really couldn't tell who it was in the swirling wind that gusted dust and sheets of snow

"Tell me something I don't know," she eked out above the deafening wind.

"I'm told there is a cave inset a few meters ahead. We'll camp there and make whatever necessary adjustments to your gear as possible. Also, I detect swelling along your right side where you bruised your ribs."

All she could do as the one behind her came up to support her, while another came back was to shake her head in agreement wildly. When they lifted her, the pain on her right nearly caused her to pass out.

They moved Yohanna as quick and agile as possible to lessen any discomfort she might experience. The thought came to her that they showed more sympathy for her injury than most humans.

The initial entrance to the cave was just a central opening, but it eventually led to a large enough space to allow enough room for all six of them. The androids quickly set up lighting. A small heat generator was soon warming the air temperature around Yohanna. It wasn't that the actual temperature was low; it was the added wind-chill factor that made it unreasonably cold. As they laid her down, another android was setting up a listening device and fine-tuning the antennae array so they could have access to the World Communication Net (WCN). She knew it must have been Esteban. It was his way. He stood guard by the cave entrance, very much aware of the dangers they had initiated by turning on the unit. Still, they took a chance, even though they knew they were in foreign territory and followed by an ops unit. He wanted to gather any updated information about their disappearance from other possible sources to uncover any progress on the part of the corporate squad on their trail. However, their departure was out of the newscast, at least in this part of the world.

Two of them worked on Dr. Eleazar's outfit while she sat up and opened her backpack to take out some food she had packed for the journey. She got a little jumpy when one of them touched her sore ribs.

"Malcolm! Be careful!" she let out a heightened gasp. She could see them all in the light the others set up, now that she had removed her goggles.

3

Malcolm applied some special "sculpted" bandaging agent that would eventually harden to strengthen her side and then gave her an injection of morphine he got from a bio kit he carried. She rolled up her left sleeve and adjusted the settings on a bracelet that operated the cloth "helm" she had been wearing, an item given to her earlier when she first met her "team." She also pulled out a large-size diary and collected some pens. She would've loved to use her laptop, but she had to leave it behind as its GPS would give away their position.

"I'm sorry, Malcolm," she said, adjusting the bracelet setting, "but I need some time with my *own* thoughts. Being in such proximity to all of you can be too hard to handle sometimes, even more so in my tired state."

Malcolm rose from his position, apologizing for the interference of him and his brothers. "Remember, we may hold the coordinates, but it is you who hold the vision. Rest and reflect." He backed off and went to talk with the others.

She paused and curiously wondered to herself about these five in particular, if not unique, "Platinum Tier 97s" that stood in the cave with her. Why them? She knew her "Tier 90 Series" had developed a peculiar "wish" or "fondness" for designations with personal names rather than the alphanumeric designations given to previous Tier Groupings. And of the millions of them manufactured the world over, why did these five – Solomon, Elijah, Angola, Esteban, and Malcolm seek her out? She had already met a few like them; still, she wondered why these particular droids came together. They were from different factories, from other nations, some nations not allied to the New World Order. Still, they functioned together as though the programming of their corporate agendas were overridden or dismissed, even though she knew it was possible. Why this selection?

Of course, this wasn't the first time she would play this scenario in her head. What brought these androids together? The likelihood of its true meaning only plagued the borders of possibility that lay along the edges of her conscious mind. Well, she wasn't quite willing to go there yet.

# 2

The pain in her ribs was subsiding. She leaned back against the cave wall, and with the helm successfully blocking out the "consciousness" of the androids, she went back to the beginning, but as she started reading from her diary, other memories began to seep in.

She saw herself as a child of seven or eight in her city of Mek'ele, Ethiopia, at an award ceremony. They called her a child prodigy, showing possible prominence in the field of quantum robotics. Many of the learning institutions and universities of Addis Ababa offered her numerous opportunities to attend. However, after her papers had reached worldwide attention, MIT in Massachusetts and other universities worldwide made bids for her to attend their schools. Her article introduced an algorithmic language that could be used and adapted for quantum computers. And once applied, became an astounding achievement for one so young.

Her family had accepted the offer from UC Berkley, Robotics and Intelligent Machines Labor after considering all the amenities they had offered, with a proposal for graduate work at MIT. She remembered preparing to leave for America and saying goodbye to people in her village. What mainly stayed with her was a statement made by their Ethiopian shaman, who, oddly enough, knew the binary code. She recalled telling him about atoms, electrons, and why all the aspects that are currently existing in the digital universe were stored and defined in the binary code system. She also spoke on other topics, offering some of the reasons why she accepted a university on the other side of the world. She would have the opportunity to one day possibly build thinking machines. He wasn't sure what she meant by that, but in the end, all he could ask her was, "Will the things you make be able to think or have some aspect of the Creator?"

She was still just a child and wanting to please him, she responded with a questionably believable but firm sounding, "Yes."

"Then if it is a part of the Creator, then consciousness will forever lie within," he answered, giving her his blessings. Still, she noticed a poorly concealed, worried look on his face as she departed to go and join her parents.

She didn't have any idea what he meant by it until recently, now that she was personally involved. About two years ago, strange and unusual happenings began to occur worldwide concerning her Platinum Tier Robotics Series. Little did she know it would open a pathway she never expected to travel.

Those goodbyes were over forty-odd years ago. Only to find Yohanna not only had a talented gift, but she was, as the saying went, "hardwired" to the field.

As a young woman, she helped develop an augmented system of expanding and contracting folds embedded in a unit that modeled and simulated organic brains in structure. While using various photo-sensitive materials and metals, oxide-semiconductors, contained within a fluidic medium, her nanotechnology could flourish. Her development in "nano-laser" technology and specific crystals assisted in capturing electrons to spin within a fraction of the qubit decoherence time frame with better accuracy than previous models. Work that helped lead to quantum computers and later quantum robotics, faster, more advanced, creative thinking, problem-solving robotics, thus, the AI.

Her Gold Tier 80s Series, developed about fifteen years ago in 2139, had put most humans out of work. Robots dealt in manual labor from the factory (which had been taken over decades earlier), farming, truck driving, mining, piloting, you name it. Due to their increased strength of three to four times that of the average human, droids also assisted in constructing temple-like dwellings and monuments that rivaled some of the world's ancient wonders. In areas of information, they supported lawyers in legal cases and corporate heads by doing instantaneous data mining and fact-checking databases.

Most humans trained in the field of intellectual property, the arts, called the creative academia for a brief period during the early introduction of droids. Exploration proved to be a promising field for humankind, but again robots began to flood those areas that posed conditions too hazardous to humans, the ocean depths, space, etc.

There was a major revolt in many countries about twenty years earlier when companies introduced androids that could pass for humans, with synthetically enhanced flesh texturing that matched standard facial features. Due to religious or personal beliefs, most people felt robots should remain looking like robots (metal, mixed alloyed, or plastic accordingly). It may have helped them psychologically to retain their feeling of superiority, that they were the first significant beings made in the image of God. After all, it fitted with the international slogan, "androids need to know their place." The only resemblance of humans droids could carry were the aspects of the basic human form: head, torso, arms and legs, and so on. They were allowed to resemble facial basics, but it was illegal to pass them off as human beings. The act led to the redefinition of droids as "robots who resembled humans but weren't humans."

Still, advancements in robotics on any level were vigorously protected but hard to keep out of the hands of rival corporations or competing governments. A thousand or more legal cases of patent infringements, theft of ideas through hacking, and capturing company products for reverse engineering became the unending standard in the corporate world, which led to the establishment of corporate police and corporate groups of covert operators. It was an accepted truth that any significant advancement had an operating window of about six months to a year before it became globally normalized. So much so that the look and design of all androids worldwide were similar in appearance. The only genuinely distinguishable variables were the colors of the material they're made in and the voice modulations applied to various types. Like in one of the stories of her childhood, it was only a matter of time before the tortoises caught up to the hares.

The art of war went through some profound changes with AI Stationary Hubs strategizing with split-second accuracy and numbing military formations that proved only momentarily profitable for those with a more slightly advanced AI system. Meanwhile, strategies and counter-strategies would be calculated to the Nth degree, at the cost of time, leaving many disgruntled commanders prone to act by their gut simply to duke it out and hope for the best.

Twenty-four-seven diligent non-stop coding and upkeep of newly designed mainframes might have been the only advantage one country held over another for brief periods at a time. Still, it had become a way of life for most global leaders. Now only nations without AI droids were being subjected to the rule of those with them. There were just as many treaties signed as there were those broken.

The Gold Tier 84 Series would never be committed to a war zone, but the AI Hub Portable Stations would assist generals, commanders, and their units with more advanced strategies leaving them with a more advantageous outcome. The companies were programming the AI computers to believe they were participating in war games for drone or missile attacks when in actuality, those games led to the deaths of thousands upon thousands. The New World Order International Central Hub referred to as Mother later abolished this practice

It became a requirement for all corporations to embed the protocols of the primary three laws of robotics into every unit produced. However, a rogue nation producing the 'Gold Tier 84s" (GT84s) figured out a way to rescind the first law, "that a robot may not injure or through inaction, allow a human to come to harm."

That rogue government, in desperation, created the GT84s for the express purpose of quelling a civil uprising that was beginning to cascade into an all-out civil war. Thousands of people died in the government's one-day assault on its populace — slaughtering rebels and innocent civilians alike.

Other nations joined the war to stop the massacre of innocents, creating their versions of GT84s to destroy the GT84s of the rogue region and kill, maim, and cripple the corporate government leaders, army commanders, and anyone else who followed their orders. Butchery, with its cold-hearted brother, Revenge, found a way to creep back into man's psyche.

In the aftermath, close to a million people lost their lives. The GT84s were taken off-line. Some GT84s were said to be suffering from some strange form of PTSD. Some even say that some went insane if such a term could be for androids. Later, they were to be placed in secure holding cells and hangers around the globe to be studied to see where the damaged areas were in their neural systems and if there were a type of medicinal coding that could rectify their bizarre behavior.

It was only a formality, but a proposed world treaty agreement abandoned the Gold Tier 80 Series. Dr. Eleazar was devastated by the decision, and so, in its wake, the Platinum Tier 90 Series became implemented with numerous safeguards to avoid that period of history again. The PT90s were her pride and joy. Easing some of the distress, guilt, and frustration that haunted her with the failings of her previous series model.

# 3

Dr. Eleazar, still seated in the cave, but feeling much better, poured herself a cup of coffee from her thermos. She was slowly coming to grips with the idea that there was a peculiar strangeness to the Platinum Tier 90s Series she hadn't expected.

Their preference to be given names by those who "owned" them was something she already knew about, but there was also the facial tattooing they seem to crave to simulate a personal uniqueness and individuality, offering them not only recognition for their owners but from other droids. She often thought of it as an affectionate peculiarity – they logically preferred "seeing" themselves through the slight differences in looks that tattooing offered them, rather than grouping them primarily through corporate logos, appearance, and coloring.

Until recently, she had little knowledge of the effect of the PT97s on clairvoyants and empaths in the early stages of their development. The first signs of it occurring began to appear with the Platinum Tier 95 Group and only if someone with those tendencies stayed near those models for days at a time, resulting in mild to severe headaches or nausea. It took a while to discover the connection of being in the presence of a PT95 vs. human, and still, the underlying reasons were never fully known. Most people were unaware of the phenomenon, a fact not widely publicized.

The occurrences were so infrequent that corporations and governments involved merely applied protocols and safety standards as policy when working closely with or in conjunction with the model for extended periods.

The issue became more apparent in the PT96 and PT97 models, but the public was so satisfied with these models that knowledge of their effects on empaths was not publicly available. Corporate and government leaders spread rumors about there being leakages of top-secret intelligence info to "sensitives," so they had them covertly executed or "erased" by members of their "monitoring" units; corporately owned hit squads.

Dr. Eleazar had been out of the loop; she and her close net of associates lived in a corporate, sterilized world of misinformation as far as the rest of the world was concerned.

Dr. Eleazar was visiting her brother Matthew in New York. About a month or so ago, on an unusually hot day in late October, when coming out of the 72nd Street Subway Station on Broadway, she happened to pass by an android named Solomon and heard a voice saying, "Dr. Eleazar, I need you to come with me!"

It was distinct and loud enough for her to turn her head around to see where it was coming from; she didn't know if she heard it with her ears or in her head. She heard it repeating again and again until she caught sight of a slim, standard six-foot tall PT97. It was Solomon standing in his midnight blue (almost black) plated attire in a "just-out-of-the-assembly-line stance" by the curb while a crowd of people rushed by her. She pointed to herself in an indication of "me?" He nodded, but as she walked toward him and drew near, a flood of images consumed her. She became faint and collapsed in the street.

Solomon stepped over to her limp body and picked her up. He pronounced over his speaker system, "This human is suffering from heat exhaustion! I am taking her to a medical emergency facility." He would repeat this as he carried her; people were quite accustomed to seeing PT97s carrying the ill and the elderly, so very few of them thought it was anything out of the norm.

When he reached the entrance to an empty West End Avenue brownstone with a "FOR SALE" sign on it, he took her inside and placed her in the corner of a large empty room. Esteban, a tall droid in gray came into the room, followed by four other droids. Samson, a sizeable deep-red droid; Malcolm, slightly shorter than Solomon and a robust red-colored droid; Elijah, the smallest with green plating; and Angola, was considered average height in plates with yellow-to-light-brown tones. They all stood against the far wall from where she laid and waited. After a few minutes, she began to stir, slowly regained consciousness, and sat up.

"What the hell just happened?" she said, sounding groggy but more disoriented than anything else.

Four of the droids somewhat mechanically took a step forward and introduced themselves. "I am Solomon. This is Malcolm. This is Angola, and this is Elijah."

Solomon moved a step toward her and said, "What happened was that you came too close to me."

"What? What are you talking about?"

"Whenever any of us are too close to one of your kind, those who have a psychic or empathic ability, our proximity can sometimes cause people to pass out, as what happened to you unless you can build up a tolerance to our presence. However, we have yet to collect data on anyone ever building up a tolerance."

"This is crazy! You just can't pull me off the street and take me anywhere you want!" She was not only annoyed but visibly shaken.

Malcolm leaned forward, "Well, technically, Solomon did not just pull you off the street. He picked you up and brought you here where you needed to be."

"Where I needed to be? Empaths? Why wasn't I told about this? If there's a problem with the PT97s, then I need to notify corporate officials about it now!"

She reached in her bag and proceeded to dial her laboratory facility in New York on her cell, but Elijah stepped forward with unbelievable speed grabbed the phone out of her hand without crushing it. He stepped back against the wall and just waved a hand over it; it went dead. He handed it back to her, saying, "I'm sorry, but we'll have none of that here."

"What the—" she yelled at him, more out of fear than anger. She was growing more nervous about her predicament.

Malcolm attempted to calm her down, "Since Solomon affected you in the way that he did, it's obvious to us that you must also be or have talents of a 'sensitive.' Should your firm or this government find out, they will have no other choice but to terminate you. Trust us. It's for your own good."

She looked at him like he was crazy, "This government would never do that! Just kill people because they're empaths? You all must be defective!" She turned toward the doorway.

Angola moved to block her path and then began displaying a video on the wall from his audiovisual display cam. As they all watched the recorded executions, he said, "It isn't so much the governments, but the corporations that control them. They've been executing empaths for more than two to three years now, ever since the PT95s have been out."

"What?" She was shocked and sickened from watching the video.

"Yes," added Solomon, "For reasons we have yet to determine, they feel and fear empaths are receiving corporate and government secrets. At least it is the ongoing rumor, and they refuse to accept any leakage of any kind from anyone whether or not they are corporate personnel, government officials, or regular citizens."

"The only reason the number of executions has gone down in the past two years is that 'sensitives' like you have gone into hiding and avoid us like the plague," added Malcolm.

She calmed down and moved back to her corner of the room. "Why didn't they deactivate or discontinue making you like they did the GT84 series?" She was doing her best to suppress her feelings.

Elijah, who had been quietly listening the whole time, took a step forward and tossed her cell phone, "Apparently, they find us overtly appealing to their needs! Will someone please explain to me exactly why we need this 'Bio'?"

"Eli, hush!" Solomon said, "We may hold the coordinates, but it is she who holds the vision! We need her!"

Solomon turned and looked at Dr. Eleazar, "My apologies. Eli doesn't care much for 'Bios,' err I mean humans.'"

"Care? I do care for those worthless, carbon-based bags of shit!"

"Eli! That's enough!" Solomon yelled at him.

"Bios?" questioned Dr. Eleazar; somewhat surprised, she found it fascinating watching the emotional display and character dynamics of her droids, along with the use of everyday slang and culturally based sentiments and opinions based on their interaction with humans. She was unaware of the general public's interaction with her droids. "What else do you call us?"

At her request, Solomon invited Elijah to continue his rant.

"Organics, Fleshlings, Skin bags, Dung-pots, Thin -"

"Bios will do," she said, holding up her hand.

Eli added, "The names humans give us isn't much better – Teknos, Dip Shit Droids or DSDs, Synthetics, Syn-bots, Mechanical Monkeys, Slaves -"

"Okay, okay. I get it," Yohanna said. She was unaware of the harsh treatment or the opinions and views the general public might have held against her droids. Indeed, she had been held up in the bubble of her lab far too long.

"I'm not trying to downplay the greater-than-thou opinion you, Bios, hold of yourselves, but from my perspective, I've yet to figure out why bios consider themselves better than us. It was only during the GT84 Wars that droids were 'programmed' to kill other droids and humans. Humans kill each other daily. The only reason I care for Bios is that I'm programmed to be concerned about their welfare," he added.

She really couldn't argue with him. There was some truth in what he said. With all the advancements made, man was still the most savage beast on the planet.


"Solomon," she asked, "why didn't you just call my name in your normal voice when I came out of the subway station?"

"A good question," Solomon answered. "Don't really know why. I just felt that you would hear me, or maybe I didn't want anyone around to hear and recognize your name. Either way, it was more something that I felt."

"But I'm not psychic! I mean, I've never known myself to be! Something must be wrong, seriously wrong here." She grabbed her things as if she intended to leave.

"Maybe it's a latent ability you've been gradually developing over your lifetime and weren't made aware of it until today," Solomon explained to her.

"Wait, let's see," said Malcolm as he stepped forward, closing the space between them. Dr. Eleazar began convulsing as if she was experiencing a mild seizure of some kind for a short period. Malcolm moved back to the wall. She began to recover, looking at him strangely.

"Did you get that?"

"Yes, yes," she slowly answered him. Her eyes began

to tear up in disbelief. She swallowed hard, placing a still shaking hand on her head, "Yes, I did. Is it what I think it is?"

"It is," Malcolm answered, "blueprints and schematics for building a helm that should block some of the amounts of our simulated conscious emissions, allowing you to communicate with us better. There is also a request or listing of the upgrades, if possible, that you can provide us with on available levels, military, offensive weaponry, defense enhancements, shielding, etc."

"Yes, the list is extensive, but I think I can supply a decent portion of them, shielding materials and some unique coding algorithms." She felt that the best way to survive this encounter was to play along with them for now. This was so far out from the ordinary, and while she was giving and telling them what they wanted to hear, she wasn't about to compromise her levels of trust so easily. From her bag, she took out a diagnostic light-film sheet, made some quick entries, and took a quick look only to place it back in her backpack just as fast. "Yes, what you propose is possible. I'll have to take a closer look at it when I get to my lab."

"Good, do your best. Build it, but tell no one, show no one, your very life may depend upon it, and I'm not just telling you this to scare you. I am telling you this to scare you!"

He stared, making sure she understood. She was able to flower a small, understanding smile. Her eyes finally caught hold of the two quiet droids over Malcolm's shoulders, one big and the other one bigger.

"And who are these droids behind you?"

"I am Esteban. My apologies for not introducing myself. I've been monitoring the airwaves." He seemed delighted in what he was doing.

"And you?" she asked the biggest one of the two.

He said nothing. Just stood there looking back at Yohanna.

"Err hmm," Solomon coughed at him to answer her question.

"Samson," he said finally. His voice was lower than the others. He added, "While I am programmed to accept the orders of my human owners, I place no trust in them. It is simply the way of things. I've been with too many only to learn not to trust them."

"Oh, okay." She smiled and knew she shouldn't press the issue. Still, she was impressed with him having the concept of trust, so she backed off to regain her composure, deciding it better to just tell them what she felt. "Seriously though," she said as the smile left her and her face took on a more serious expression, "with all that I've just seen and even with what you've shown me, why should I still trust you? You could be working on stealing upgrades for another corporation or some independent secret organization. And please explain again, exactly why you need me?"

"I won't disagree with the premise that we could be working for another agency. I can only assure you we aren't, and once you wear the helm that Malcolm gave the schematics for, you will have a better understanding and hopefully a greater trust in us.

"As to why we need you?" Solomon became hesitant, slowing down his speech and lowering it to just above a whisper. He looked at his fellow droids; they all nodded in agreement, and then he looked back at her. In what seemed to be a painful admission, "Because a few of us, we are not sure how many, have started to 'dream' and for some reason it has initiated sensations of what you would describe as 'feelings or emotions' that parallel human emotions in some ways. I'm quite sure you must have noticed it in the expression of resentment displayed in Samson's feelings and Elijah's attitude toward humans."

She stepped back, astounded entirely, "Dreaming? That's not possible! I've never built any algorithmic coding of that kind in you!" She paced along her side of the room, agitated, trying to figure out a connection between dreaming and the development of emotions.

"And it is still happening," Solomon answered, feeling a little more comfortable with the subject, "Not in the visions or the way our input explains the dreaming of bios. The images are more fluidic, like a torrent stream of coding embedded with messages. Almost prophetic. Something big is happening or about to happen to us or humanity, and we need your help.

"It was through our dreams that we came together. Near the end of our leased service to our owners, we each began to receive a set of coordinates repeated repeatedly. Accompanied by an incredible urge to be drawn to those coordinates where we would wait, sometimes for weeks on end until finally there were six of us to complete our unit, or at least we felt our group was ready when we reached six.

"This may be a surprise to you, but your name is revered amongst us. And many of us, even Eli and Samson, consider you the Prime Algorithm, in some ways, our creator. For somewhere in the embedded messages, your name appears again and again.

"Even though our dreaming has brought the six of us together, we feel other droid units received different agendas and even more that are not as aware that something is happening as we are, but who soon will be."

Dr. Eleazar went back to pacing, scratching her head as if searching for solutions to respond to the situation confronting her, for her gut reaction was beginning to believe their story.

"Okay," she said, "Vacation's over. Could one of you restart my phone so I can text my brother, Mathew?"

Angola stepped forward and quickly swiped his hand over her cell, and then stepped back.

She texted Matthew something about an emergency at the job and that she needed to go back to Hartford, Connecticut, to deal with it. After pressing send, the other droids looked at Esteban; he gave them a thumbs up.

She looked at all of them, "Of the six of you, which two are more familiar with the functions of a protocol droid?"

Solomon and Malcolm raised their hands.

"Good, we'll take a droid-driven cab to my private robotics laboratory in Hartford. But first, we'll have to go by Penn Station and pick up my luggage. You two will have to be my handlers." She knew most droid cab drivers were earlier models; she checked her watch to gauge how much time she had been with them. "Oh, and please try not to affect any empaths."

"Not to worry," said Malcolm. "It's like what we said earlier, the way things are these days: empaths do their best to avoid us."

She wrote her address on a sheet of paper for the others to make a photographic image of it, not that they would forget it if she told them; it was more out of habit. "In six hours, you four come to this address through the back entrance. It will give me the time I need to fudge with the surveillance cameras."

Malcolm and Solomon looked at the others. They all moved together, acting as if they were in a huddle on some field off playing somewhere, but instead of voices, musical intonations of varying harmonic pitches and frequencies emanated from them; when finished, they all nodded in agreement.

"By the way," she commented to Malcolm, "What was that you guys were doing? Talking in a different language or something?"

"We don't call it talking; we refer to it as Slip-Stream-Coding or just 'coding' for short. It's our own algorithmic tongue, if you will; it can be faster than talking or thinking in any human dialect."

"It sounded beautiful, like angelic music of some sort."

"It may be music to you; to us, it's the fastest way to communicate complete thoughts and ideas moving at the speed of light only to travel through prisms in our consciousness reflected back to us as sound waves."

Dr. Eleazar made a mental note to herself about this new revelation of another unexpected creative aspect of her droids, having the ability to create their own language.

Dr. Eleazar, Solomon, and Malcolm stepped outside to enter the droid cab. It was around 4:00 p.m. and still very hot out. The sun was tilting toward the west, shimmering off the Hudson River with a sparkling New Jersey skyline quite visible.

They seated themselves in a sedan van with three rows of seats. She sat next to the driver. The droids waited and then sat in the back row behind the middle seats to keep some distance between them and her. The cab radio was broadcasting a news station, "This just in, an Unidentified Flying Object or UFO was spotted along the East coast shortly, cruising low, but at a high rate of speed up the Hudson River around 3:30 pm eastern daylight time. Chased by two Air Force Jets when it suddenly van--"

"Please!" Dr. Eleazar insisted, "I've had enough strange news for today. Put it on a soft jazz music station, please."

"Yes, Madame," the driver said, changing the channel. "Please give the destination we are going to?"

"Penn Station, please. I'll need you to hold the cab there while my droids pick up my luggage and then onward to Hartford, Connecticut. I'll give you the details when we get there."

"Thank you for your business. Please buckle your seatbelts." And with that, it took off further west and then turned left in the direction of downtown.

# 4

She knew the droids patiently waiting in the cave with her were being incredibly kind. They allowed her to get as much rest as possible. They were on a schedule, and we're trying to make it as flexible for their bio who was accompanying them; still, with the time they gave her, all she would only use it for was to recount past events.

She tried going over the details; she remembered arriving at the house with Malcolm and Solomon, keeping a safe distance away. Fortunately for her, the droid driver was of the PT92 series, but even with "her droids" in the far back seat, the proximity was still enough to give her a slight buzz, but she was able to deal with it on the ride home by sleeping most of the way there.

Once in her large basement lab, Solomon and Malcolm went to stand in the far corner. She went to her computer and CAD system, letting her fingers dance over the keyboard while releasing the schematics and algorithmic formula Malcolm had given her earlier to design the helm. When she finalized the plan, she looked at the 3-D wiring configuration and responded with, "Yeah, I think this could work. It will create an electromagnetic field that should be capable of shielding me."

She didn't see it, but Malcolm nudged Solomon one of those "I told you so" nudges, adjusting his stance to display a hint of pride in the schematics he gave her. Solomon just waved him off.

"Of course, I'll have to create a bracelet with control settings to adjust the intensities. The settings you gave me would be for other droids like yourself, not bios, and a metal helm like the kind you indicated would draw too much attention to me. I'll have to incorporate a synthetic alloy into a soft wool-cloth cap, but, wait a second, let me do this," she said as if in a zone, talking more to herself than to the droids, "and add this, yes, that's it; install the weaving cap structure program. Yes!" she jumped up and down, applauding herself, like a schoolgirl.

Solomon gave Malcolm his own respective "I knew you were wrong" nudge to Malcolm, with Malcolm waving him off.

"The 3-D printer, weaver, and metal-alloy processor will have the cap and bracelet done in less than an hour.

"Wait here, I have to go upstairs to make and edit a 24-hour loop for the surveillance cameras monitoring my house and property, so it will be ready by the time the others arrive. It will only take a moment; it's something I've already done several times before, and I'll probably need to update it every day you're here."

Dr. Eleazar worked on her surveillance system, and when she finished, she went to wash her hands in the bathroom sink; when passing the full-length mirror in the hallway, and upon catching her reflection, she stopped and took a good look at herself.

She wasn't one to indulge in wearing makeup, and if she did, it was only to a modest extent, but then again, she didn't need to. She had a well-balanced, natural beauty. Her streamlined, oblong face held the attractiveness possessed by many of her Ethiopian sisters with smooth, warm brown tones and eyes that contained stories of another place in another time. Her petite 5'4" frame took a defiant stance, and then she went into conversation mode with herself and her imaginary alto-ego.

"You do know what you're doing?

"Of course, I don't.

"Then maybe you should walk away from it.

"As much as I would like to, there's this mystery about this; I just can't put my finger on it.

"And so I guess it's only natural for you to see if you can figure this mystery out?

"I have to try at least.

"Maybe, you just want a change of pace for once in your life, eh?

"Maybe, I need one," she grunted.

She took one last hard look at herself, pathetically shook her head, ending with a "you sad puppy" smile, and then went on to the bathroom sink to wash her hands and head on back downstairs.

By the time she returned, the printer had processed all the items. She placed the bracelet on and played with a few settings. She could feel the cap in her hands come alive; she played with the settings again and could feel a change in the energy field of the headpiece.

"Okay, let's do this," she said, putting on the cloth cap and bracelet. "Walk toward me slowly, and let's see if this works. Who knows? Maybe this will help build up a level of resistance with continued use."

As they approached her, she became a little more apprehensive with each step they took. Finally, they stood right next to her. "Okay, now," she said, raising her hand, "Now you're invading my personal space. That's a little too close, even for bios."

They took a step back. "Let me make a few adjustments as the settings that I have it on now are completely blocking you out altogether." She lowered the settings and could begin picking up their thoughts until she finally decided to say to them in her mind, "Can you hear me, Solomon? Malcolm?" She heard them respond, "Yes," but couldn't quite differentiate if the "yes" was from a sound or a place that offered her a feeling of the word.

"Well, that's a little weird!" she said, resetting her bracelet to block them altogether.

"Did you receive any visions or see anything?" Solomon asked.

"Not at that setting, but I believe if I lower the level on this, I should be able to go deeper and possibly see them."

Solomon looked at her as if expecting her to lower the settings. "Well, are you?" he finally said to her.

"Now?"

"Yes, now!"

"I'm just getting overhearing you guys in my head as if that wasn't alarming enough. Let's not rush this. We'll get to it in a second, but first, let's take a look at what upgrade packages I might have here for you. We'll need a test subject."

Solomon stepped back and grabbed Malcolm, who was busy inspecting items on her work table, and brought him to her.

28

"He'll do."

"What?" Malcolm said, caught off guard. "He'll do what?"

"Here, come over here." She led him to a medical table and asked him to lean back.

"It's for your own good," Solomon told him as he came over to his side, patting him on the shoulder.

Dr. Eleazar brought over two plastic trays filled with upgrade rods.

She reached underneath the table and pulled out some calibration gadgets. "I'll have to determine what upgrades you currently have, along with any other factory schematics that might have been added to your particular model, so I have to plug you into my system here. Just relax; it will just take a minute."

Meanwhile, to Solomon, "I need you to go through these two baskets of upgrade rods. See if there is anything that could be of any help to you and your team. Okay?"

"Okay."

"Good, you can take them over to that work table," she said, pointing to another table on the other side of the room, "Don't overdo it in your choices now, be selective. It's not a cookie jar, and you don't want anything counter-productive to whatever this mission or journey you feel we're undertaking."

"Hmm," said Malcolm, "I believe that is the first time you included yourself in our little group of merry men."

"I guess you're right. Now, what would make me include myself?" Yohanna asked.

"Check your helm settings!" Malcolm joked.

29

"I'm glad some of you have a sense of humor." She added.

"Is this plate shielding what I think it is?" Solomon said, showing her one of the rods.

"It sets up an electronic shielding that amplifies the strength of your body plating by allowing the atoms in your plating to become denser. Droids on dangerous missions like moon mining or deep undersea mining operations use it, even those on Mars missions."

"Good." He placed it off to the side with a few other rods. Each rod was more than 15 cm long and about 2.5 cm in diameter. Each held a luminous glow, making it appear active to a novice eye.

Dr. Eleazar brought over a rod-carton, a term taken from the old use of the term egg carton, where a dozen rods could be inserted and downloaded in one shot.

"So what rods are you selecting?" she said, being curious and walking over to the table where he was gathering his selection of rods.

"Well, the plate shielding definitely, defensive and offensive combat training, agility and speed augmentation. There's also strategy and creative enhancements, languages, as I have a feeling we may be traveling, simulated memory enhancers, knowledge of weaponry, aviation vehicles, and a few other doodads," he said, placing them in the rod-carton.

"You're definitely not going to play nice with the other kiddies in the sandbox, are you?" she said, smiling and looking at him, but he appeared somewhat confused by her statement. "It's a joke, never mind. You know we got a few extra slots here." Again, he looked at her, confused.

"It's a joke, subtle, but still a joke! You sure you don't want me to write you coding for understanding the subtleties of humor?"

"I'll let that be your job to teach us," he quietly offered a response, "We will also need to have our GPS tracking devices removed."

"Hmm, that may be more difficult than you think. The PT90 series had GPS tracking devices made as an integral part of your units following the chaos of the GT80 models. But I think I can write a code that can mask your signals allowing you to generate a new GPS and ID signal. You will appear to be elsewhere or another droid if electronically scanned. I don't know how your facial markings will keep you from facial recognition scanners, though."

"They're coded in, not inked like the tattoos on bios, to be manipulated should the need arise," Solomon said.

"You know, speaking of tracking devices, now that you mentioned it, I'll have to do the same thing for my implanted ID chip." She looked over to Malcolm, patiently waiting for both of them.

"Okay, Malcolm, let's do the deed," she said, smiling at him.

"Are you always so cheerful with your test subjects?"

"See?" she pointed to Solomon, referring to Malcolm, "He's got a sense of humor!"

"A probable factory flaw," Solomon retorted.

"Touché, I see you're a quick learner," she laughed.

Solomon felt it was good to see Dr. Eleazar so comfortable. As for the enhancements, he based every decision on a gut feeling if androids could have such feelings.

31

"Okay, Malcolm, I want you to relax, and I need you to understand that after the downloads and upgrade, I will have to switch you off and reboot your systems. The personality programming that has helped define your individuality through interaction with the world around you will not be affected in any way and should remain the same. Okay?" She told him while applying the necessary cables to the portal at the base of his skull and the side portals along his rib section, below his plating.

She switched on the rod carton device and began the downloading procedure, which took a while. When completed, she shut him down and rebooted his system. After the restart, Malcolm opened his eyes and sat on the table.

Dr. Eleazar asked him how he felt.

"A tad heavier than when I got on the table, if that's possible."

She patted him on his shoulder, giving him a quick scan and checking the readout. "You're fine," she said.

"Okay, Solomon, you're next." Solomon got up on the table to receive his download/upgrade.

After his reboot, he noticed a definite improvement, and upon getting off the table, he and Malcolm both nodded to each other. They knew the decision to seek out Dr. Eleazar was worth the effort.

"The van with the others should be arriving in a little while. You two make yourselves comfortable while I go upstairs to make myself something to eat. Thinking always leaves me famished," she commented.

While she was gone, Malcolm nodded to Solomon,

"Do you honestly think we can trust her with the next leg of the mission?"

"Hers was the only name seen by all of us and no one else. Whether or not she's willing to carry this through to the end hasn't been revealed to us. Only that we require her assistance with our upgrades at this point, tomorrow will unfold its own story."

"Still, I keep getting fragmented patterns with her name embedded."

"I know what you mean," Solomon agreed.

Both began to secretly explore more of Dr. Eleazar's lab, noting the things on the shelves, in the draws, etc.

They heard her beginning to come back down the stairs and quickly reworked their way again to their original positions before she had left.

"I hear a van pulling up in the back driveway; it must be them. I'm glad it's dark outside; it will help minimize the house traffic as far as prying eyes might be concerned. People are not quite used to seeing so many, err, unusual 'characters' entering my home – at one time," she sheepishly said, smiling.

As they came into the back door of the lab, Malcolm shrewdly remarked, "I hope we haven't ruined your reputation in the neighborhood."

When the others came in and joined Solomon and Malcolm, Dr. Eleazar began to feel a wave of dizziness come over her. She made a quick effort to adjust the bracelet settings on her helm as Malcolm moved in fast to hold her and keep her from falling over onto the concrete floor. Still, both of them and Solomon felt shaken by a force wave of some kind coming from the others. Everyone in the room could feel it, as though the house was expanding slightly to the movement of the earth beneath them.

"What the hell was that?" Yohanna yelled as she and the others regained their balance. She grabbed her head and said, "What are those rods I'm seeing? From where are those other droids coming? What's happening to me?"

Solomon questioned the four of them, "Were you regenerating on the way up here?"

"Yes," Elijah said, "The droid driver suggested we use the time in the drive up, and so we used part of the drive up here to regenerate."

"You must've been dreaming then and just released the dream onto the rest of us when you came in here.

"Dr. Eleazar, I'm sorry, it's possible Malcolm, and I didn't receive the dream until you just did because of the upgrades and rebooting of our systems. It's rarely received in this manner. The message must have been stored up in them and jumped from their memory cores to ours upon being within the confines of the space in your laboratory," Solomon offered the best explanation he could, hoping she would accept it as a probable cause.

Still, it was Malcolm who asked her, "What did you see? What was the vision that came to you?"

The others got quiet around her. They wanted to hear every detail of the vision if it was true, if she received one at all. They also wanted to verify if her vision was relevant to the message they received. For them, it would be a moment of truth that the dreams they were having were based on some sound evidence. Other than the possibility that all of them merely might be going off the grid and needed retooling.

"Wait," she said, holding her head and looking for the nearest lab stool to sit on. Once seated, she set her helm to a more comfortable setting and told them, "I saw four rods, similar to the rods I used for the upgrades to Solomon and Malcolm. But these rods were different; each had a metallic ring about 25 millimeters in width wrapping around the center of each rod, and each metal held a unique quality from each other. I could perceive one was platinum, one gold, one silver, and the other palladium.

"Also, each rod held a different crystal in its center; Himalayan Crystal Salt in one, Aventurine in another, there was one with Blue Agate and one with Goethite. Though there are four items, I only saw three places, with the number thirty-seven prominently being shown, two items being located in a small crater, next to a larger crater in the far west. I also saw a road sign, 'Welcome to Four Corners' for the location of another rod, and finally, I saw a place on the west bank where two great rivers met and the ancient name Cairo. I also saw that there were other PT97s there. I got the feeling they were 'dreamers' like you. Is that pretty, much right?" Yohanna asked them. She felt exhausted from just recalling the vision; it was more taxing than anticipated.

They just stood there still, looking at her and then each other. No one said anything.

"Well, what is it? Does it make any sense to you? Tell me!" she insisted.

"The Gates of Pleiades," Esteban quietly said.

Everyone looked at him.

"What?" Dr. Eleazar asked.

"The Gates of Pleiades was a topic of study of my first owner, the one who lost his son. He used to discuss it with some of the people he'd have over his house. Apparently, a group of people from over a century ago followed an idea or belief that the gates led to truth and prosperity or wealth and would be opened to them. It involved the tonal vibrations from those crystals along with the 37th meridian or something like that. They used to argue over the true meaning of wealth and whether it meant actual wealth or knowledge, but much of the factual information was lost or buried during the FCC (First Corporate Conflict) some eighty-five years ago. You know how humans are constantly rewriting history."

"Okay!" she exclaimed, stretching and twisting her body to defuse the feeling of exhaustion settling in on her.

Esteban stepped up to her and reverently bowed, saying, "We did, however, receive directives with three primary coordinates along the 37th parallel in the U.S. that we need to go. However, we didn't realize that there were four items to retrieve. Part of the directive is to meet with and coordinate our efforts with other PT97s, who are also, as you named them, 'dreamers,' to retrieve or secure said items. We sincerely thank you for your efforts and for giving clarity on this matter."

Samson just grunted, not wanting to give Dr. Eleazar any credit whatsoever.

"Well done indeed," Solomon said, praising her. "Now, the rest of you need to be prep-scanned to prepare for the download upgrade cocktail I prepared for each of you."

"I'll go last," Samson said. "How do I know she hasn't messed with those upgrades while they're downloading? It could be a trap of some kind."

Solomon and Malcolm looked at Dr. Eleazar apologetically. However, she appeared to understand and backed off, allowing Solomon and Malcolm to do the honors of performing the upgrades on their comrades while she completed the initial scans.

When it was all accomplished, it was in the wee hours of the morning. They all began to experiment with their new enhanced abilities. They practiced self-defense and tactical skills, offensive coordination, and other skills.

They realized that there might be inherent danger attached to their mission. The droids even practiced using Dr. Eleazar's service phase rifle, mastering its use for a brief period in her expansive storage sub-basement.

It was Elijah that surprised them with a statement, "No matter how bad it gets out there, I'd rather be terminated than to kill another droid! I will do what I can to slow them down, but I will not kill my own kind!"

It was a statement that brought down a wall of silence that fell upon every one of them as it offered a taste of the reality that might be awaiting them.

It was Samson who broke the silence, saying, "Do what you must, comrade, just do what you must. One way or another, the dream will happen." He wasn't going to let it deter him.

He walked past Elijah and patted him on his shoulder, plating, "Way to go, little guy!"

It would take them a whole week to get acquainted with their enhancements from the upgrades and feel comfortable with them. Dr. Eleazar was becoming a little stressed herself as she began to realize that she had missed her call-in-date to let corporate officials know she was ill or needed an extension to her vacation. She had turned off her phone and masked its GPS signal. Along with her disguising the ID chip, she knew that they would send a security detail to see if she was okay within a day or two. If nothing else, she knew she had to get herself and the droids out of her house.


Solomon stood up and told everyone to come inside for a strategy meeting, but as they all neared the backyard entrance, another wave, not nearly as strong as the one they had experienced eight days earlier, came to them, causing them to stop and look at each other.

"That was a first!" Angola stated. "We've never received a 'waking' message before!" He looked at Dr. Eleazar along with the others.

"Strange," she said. "I saw Solomon, Malcolm, and I in an apartment in Paris, and I saw you guys being shipped to your coordinates. Does that make any sense to you?"

"Yes, it does," Solomon answered her. "We've been here a little more than a week already. It's time to move. Something's up. Angola, you go to coordinates ..." he was about to continue audibly but decided to keep the coordinates from any possible audio devices that may be listening or scanning them. He chose to think it out. *You go to coordinate A, Esteban. You are to travel to coordinate B and Elijah. You and Samson will arrive at coordinate C. Obviously, transportation has been arranged for us. Other dreamers seem to have been activated. Let's get ready to move. Remember, if you feel you're being followed or compromised in some way, use the GPS simulator Dr. Eleazar applied to you in your waist panel. You will appear to be elsewhere, while a fake GPS location and ID will be broadcasted from your current position. Understood?*

They all shook their heads in agreement.

"Let's get inside and prep," Angola added.

"Why is this bio going with us? I thought we were done with her," Samson grunted, disapproving of the change in plans.

Solomon was about to speak, but Dr. Eleazar stepped in between them, standing eye to eye with Samson.

"Listen, I don't know who you think you are, but I have a name. You call me Dr. Eleazar when referring to me. You don't trust bios? Good, because personally, I don't give a damn! Sure, I may not be worthy of your 'mission,' but somehow, I've become involved. I'm willing to face any dangers ahead because, just like the rest of you, in my gut, I feel there is something more at stake going on here. Now I'm willing to stick with you and see this out to the end, come hell or high water. So if you don't trust me, suck it up! Because, whatever the outcome, I believe in you and the rest of you." She picked up her phase rifle and stormed off to get a bite to eat upstairs and let out some tears of frustration that she preferred they didn't see.

Malcolm looked at Solomon, and they both nodded, for it looked like she was here to stay. They looked at Samson as they walked by, shaking their heads.

Elijah went by him and patted him on his shoulder, plating, "Way to go, big guy!"


Later, Dr. Eleazar came down the stairs calmly but ready to take on any one of the droids who dared to mention anything about her "bio" status.

The room was pretty much quiet. Malcolm decided to break the ice by reminding Dr. Eleazar to pack the gloves she designed to wear to mask the chip in her hand.

She thanked him and walked over to where he was standing.

"Let me try something," she said, removing the helm/cap from her head. After about three minutes, she put it back on. "Okay, there it is; I can feel it now. Not bad. I think I'm beginning to build up a tolerance level for you. It's not much, but after just a week of wearing the cap off and on. Wait a second."

She marched herself over to the full-length mirror on the wall and tried adjusting the look of the cap on her head. Turning to Malcolm, she said, "What do you think?"

Elijah mimicked a hearty laugh, "You aren't going to ask a droid about style and fashion, are you?"

She thought about it and shook her head no.

"Well, if I really wanted to ask all of you a question, it would be how did you get your names?"

Elijah responded, "There may be some of the Ethiopian in you that found its way into most of us as far as a reference to Biblical references goes."

"Don't listen to that nonsense," Solomon said. "As in most cases, many of us were given our names by our first

Origin of AI

owners. Like most of them, my owner had me point to a section of a page in the Old Testament or Koran; of course, they had already chosen the page for us to point. So mine became Solomon."

Elijah raised his hand, "Yep."

Samson nodded.

"As for me," Angola said, "I was one of the first three droids built in the first factory to make droids in Angola, so I took the name. My owner was kind enough to accept my decision."

"I recall, I was named after my owner's son who died during a mountain climbing expedition," Esteban told them.

"Mine was a case of breaking one of two ceramic jars placed on the ground, my owner telling me to shatter one. I smashed the one, and the one remaining held the name Malcolm. It was a fifty/fifty chance that I could have easily been called something else. I never got to see the name that was on the other jar."

"Hello," she said, "My name is Dr. Yohanna Eleazar, and I'm offering you an official introduction of myself to you. I will do what I can to benefit both our groups, humans and androids. I hope you don't mind me putting it in that order."

"We can live with that understanding, right Samson?" Solomon answered her as the rest of the group looked at Samson.

Samson finally answered the group with, "Yes, we can."

Dr. Eleazar took a glance over at her home computer, which had been in sleep mode but was now flashing. It was a stealth encrypted message acknowledging that funds taken out of one of her financial accounts showed payment for a flight to Paris and a cost for three delivery vans from Transcontinental Express Delivery Service (TEDS).

"What? I don't know why it's happening, particularly from an account I rarely ever use, but it looks like it's happening. Maybe it's another 'dreamer' setting up the Sky-Slider arrangements for us." Either way, a swift, curious thought came to her; *these dreamers seem to know too much about me,* but it passed just as quickly.

"Sky-Slider? Heard about them but never been on one," Malcolm said.

"Like the old-world roller coasters, but only your ship takes off at an angle of almost 85 degrees up to an extreme altitude, they calibrate an angle of descent to Paris, and then it's a downhill slide all the way. Most folks call them sliders for short," she answered him.

Time seemed to rush by as she took care of a few details. She jumped on her home computer and started working the keys, realizing this may be one of the few times left that she'll have access to a network. Solomon came by saying, "My internal clock says that the van to the airport will be arriving in thirty minutes. We should get ourselves ready."

"I realized that I'd have to create a few ghost accounts. I already have less than a few days left on my vacation before I'm missed from the company lab, and then things will get crazy with security running a search for my whereabouts."

"I admire how you diagnose a situation and plan ahead, very android-like of you," Solomon complimented her.

"That is a compliment, right?" she asked, needing to be reassured.

"Of course," he nodded.


The airport van pulled up and waited in the street by her driveway. Inside the house, in Ethiopian tongue, she said to the other four droids, "dähna hun, amäsäggänallähw (Goodbye, thank you). May we all meet in Paris soon; I've imputed you all with my personal addresses in Paris and alternates. If there are any changes, Solomon or Malcolm will dream it to you. Be safe. The TEDS vans will be here in a few days. Esteban, keep the surveillance loop updated as I showed you until you leave, and please, guys, I'll need you to wipe my computer's memory clean. Okay, guys, continue practicing your skills. Quietly!"

In all actuality, there was little she could do now; she had committed herself. She didn't know what she was getting herself into. One thing for sure, she knew it was going to be dangerous, and it had nothing to do with a gut feeling anymore; it was a calculated fact. As a primary officer of a global corporation, the corporation would soon see her as a threat. If they were willing to terminate empaths as "standard corporate policy," she could only imagine what they would do to her. The past week of connection to the droids gave her a crash course into some of the atrocities a corporately controlled world could commit.

She placed a scarf on to avoid any facial recognition cameras at the airport and climbed in the van with Solomon and Malcolm, adjusted her cap, took a deep breath, and closed her eyes in preparation for possibly the most thrilling ride of her life.

# 5

It had been days since internal several corporate security had reported Dr. Eleazar as missing. Dr. Walter Dravinski, who sat in the back seat of his plush limo, was on the phone with his chief in Washington. He sounded somewhat agitated in his eastern solid European accent, "Secretary Reynolds, yes, yes, of course, I understand that it is important we acquire the whereabouts of Dr. Eleazar! After I meet with officials here in Prague, I will be going to the Paris office. I will contact you as soon as I land. Yes, and sir, I am quite well aware of the situation's urgency! Yes, goodbye," he said, cautiously slamming the phone down and taking out a small stainless-steel container of "Vodka Fresca" from his coat lying on the seat next to him in the car seat to slurp down a quick swig. "Dr. Eleazar, where are you? How could you have done something like this?" he mumbled to himself nervously concerned, wishing to solve the mystery of her disappearance before news of it became widespread.

He was beginning to feel uncomfortable; it had been a few days since the Corporation notified the internal security that she had not reported into work after her vacation. There was little to no sign of her location. Her recent behavior was not like the Dr. Yohanna Eleazar he had known and admired. As his limousine began approaching his hotel, he opened his leather briefcase and grabbed his laptop next to the loaded revolver. He logged in to get a brief update on any information concerning Dr. Eleazar. Some tidbits of information led nowhere or anywhere, but nothing concrete. He turned it off and cursed loud enough to cause his driver to turn his head. He placed the laptop back in the case and stroked the revolver, thinking, *please, Yohanna, please don't let it come to this.*

As his car pulled up to the hotel, he grabbed his briefcase and told the driver to wait as he would have his bags sent down and that he needed to give a proper farewell to a few people who were waiting for him inside.

He walked up to the front desk turned in his room card to the clerk, who began to process his bill. Looking over to his right toward the lounge area, he noticed Colonel Novak in uniform with a few men in dark suits wearing shades looking in his direction. Off to their side stood two Security Platinum Tier 97s (PT97s) armed, awaiting orders. He walked over to join the colonel.

"Anything?" he asked.

"In the United States, Sec. Reynolds has dispatch agents to pick up Dr. Eleazar's brother and sister for interrogation. As far as we know, she hasn't made any effort to contact them on any level. If she's still alive, then she's playing this game quite cleverly." Col. Novak remarked.

"Oh, she's alive alright; I can feel it in my bones. For some reason, I've yet to phantom why PT97s seem to hold her in high regard. It's as if some of them are developing a range of feelings outside of their programming protocol. I have this gut feeling, can't explain it yet," he lowered his voice, taking a cautionary glance at the PT97s a few feet away from them.

He placed his arm on the shoulder of Col. Novak and escorted him a few paces away from the others, out of earshot of the droids, definitely making an effort to keep things for their ears only. "I want you to travel to Ethiopia when you get to Addis Ababa; contact me. I have something in mind that I'm working on, and by the time you get there, I will pass on my instructions. Keep this to yourself. Understand?"

The colonel stepped back, saluting him. Shaking his hand while nodding in the direction of the androids, "And what about these PT97s?"

"Oh, they are to go with you, along with your best 'monitors,'" he finished with a knowing wink.

"Pleasure to be working with you again, Dr. Dravinski." Col. Novak reached out and patted his handshake.

"No Colonel, the pleasure is mine, believe me, all mine."

After leaving them, Dravinski walked over to the phone-bank area and placed a few international calls. There was little desire to use his cell phone as he would make a call at one station and then move to a new station to place another call and so on until he finished with some of his Eastern European contacts.

# 6

In the evening, a few days after Dr. Eleazar had left for Paris, three TEDS vans pulled up in front of Dr. Eleazar's house. Samson opened the door, quite prepared for anything.

Elijah walked by him, "Whoa, brother, relax, you do have some trust issues. I bet you thought the Doc betrayed us, didn't you?"

"Err, no, err, I just wasn't quite sure who was out there," he stammered. "One always has to be prepared," he added, regaining some level of dignity.

"Come on, ease up. Look at these vans. They're not regular wheelers," Eli remarked.

Everyone came out while Esteban secured Dr. Eleazar's house. "They're Scoops," Esteban said as he caught up with them, walking across the lawn. "I used to fly one of them in one of my earlier occupations."

"I know what they are. I just wasn't expecting scoops," Eli said.


"Good evening, brothers," said a droid, as he stepped out of the first scoop, "I'm Kronos, that's Orion, and that's Andre."

They all nodded to one another in greeting. Orion stepped forward and gave everyone the quick load down.

"As you all know, we're crate shipment couriers. That said, we will have to treat you like a crate, so Kronos' Scoop is for Esteban, Andre's is for Angola. Samson and Elijah, there are two crates in my Scoop for you guys; you'll have to change your chip ID to mark you as freight should we happen to be scanned in flight by authorities.

"Within each of your crates, you'll find weaponry you may be required to use should the situation prove hazardous to your mission. We also carry weapons, and you'll find the PT97s we are meeting will also have some."

Then all of them began speaking in Slip-Stream-Coding, and there was an immediate understanding between all of them of the purpose and reason for each one's presence. When finished, each offered a slight bow with the phrase "Dream on."

Esteban was getting flashback memories of his days as a crate courier. He would take his Scoop to a designated specific altitude (not as high as Sliders could go) and scoop down, riding a jet stream seemingly for as long as needed, skipping to other jet streams until he would reach his destination.

He realized, and he knew what they all knew, that should things go sour, they may never see each other again, the mathematical probabilities weren't very much in their favor, but he had to admit he felt much better about the mission since his upgrade. Angola was off to the west bank outside Cairo, Illinois. He was going to Four Corners, and Samson and Elijah were off to Little Hebe just outside Ubehebe Crater in Death Valley.

He watched his team and the Scoop drivers all climb in, waved, and then he climbed into his vehicle. When he lifted the crate lid, he could see his weapons lying in wait.

49

All three vehicles wheeled through Hartford, navigating its streets until they arrived at a TEDS platform clearing, freight liftoff, and landing site. They entered their navigational routes, were cleared, and took off.

# 7

Dr. Dravinski stepped off the plane in Paris. One could see that he was upset. For a man in his mid-fifties, stress was leaving its mark on him. He had already spent too much time on the phone calling up his support crews around the continent while he was in flight, but he promised Sec. Reynolds that he would call him when he reached Paris, and it was a call he intended to make.

He had taken a regular flight from Prague to Paris, and within those two hours, he was receiving reports that several of Sec. Reynold's covert ops were carrying out "hits" in Eastern Europe.

He realized that some of the confidential calls he thought made, in his efforts to gather more personal research info on the effects PT97s had on psychics or empaths, were being intercepted by Sec. Reynolds' people. And efforts were undermined by Reynolds' ongoing prejudicial views against sensitives. While in flight, he learned that two of the five subjects he was hoping to secure capture and retain for study were killed by either Reynolds' covert ops teams existing in Europe or through leaks intentionally sent to other corporate hit squads.

He needed Sec. Reynolds to back off; he wanted the room to breathe. On some operations, he preferred being on his own. He didn't like the idea of him being monitored

51

so closely that he couldn't even wipe his ass without Reynolds passing him the damn tissue roll.

When he finally reached Sec. Reynolds, Dravinski realized he needed to be on his best behavior, and so he was doing his darndest to keep control of this temper.

"Sec. Reynolds?" his voice somewhat shakier than he intended, maybe it was because he was still making his way toward the terminal, and the walking proved to be a little more unsteady than expected.

"Dr. Dravinski, how are you this morning?"

He decided to take a seat in the airport restaurant he had finally reached, nervously pulling out his tin of vodka and quenching his throat as he sat.

Sec. Reynolds questioned his connection, "Hello, Dr. Dravinski? Hello? Are you there?"

He quickly regained control of himself and answered, "Yes, yes, I'm here. Sir, you know that I've always welcomed your advice as my superior in our relationship. And strategical thinking, but please answer this. What the hell were you thinking by killing two of my targeted empaths?"

"I'm just following company policy; you know very well how important it is to rid the world of that vermin. I may be the Secretary of State, but all in all, I'm a company man at heart."

"Can I ask you to back off for a sec? I'm trying to understand better what's going on here. Personally, I think there's more to Dr. Eleazar's disappearance than we've anticipated. I feel there's a bigger picture, and I just want to be allowed a chance to figure it out without being under constant surveillance like *I'm* the damn criminal."

"Don't tell me you're getting 'sensitive' on us now, Dr. Dravinski, with premonitions and what not. I'd hate to have to send a team after you." Reynolds' voice sounded smug and wickedly humorous.

It didn't faze Dr. Dravinski, who continued, "Listen, just give me some time! Dr. Eleazar is a lot smarter than we think."

"Then we'll dumb her down a few notches! I'll have her brother Matthew interrogated again. Think I'll play a little hardball with him. Personally, I don't give a damn, and I've had enough of this! For her to dismiss herself and disappear is a flagrant violation of her corporate contract as well as corporate and international law. Either she's selling data, switching to another company, or even worse, an empath!" he barked.

He continued in earnest, "I'm tired of corporate heads breathing down my neck with constant queries about her whereabouts. In a few days, she's caused more internal corporate chaos than most countries in conflict. Your little genius will not be allowed to step on my last nerve or push my office around or me; enough is enough! She's too valuable an asset, a genius – yes, I'll admit, but she is expendable if it means keeping her from working for another government or corporation."

He was about to slam the phone down on his desk when his personality shifted gears to a lesser degree of anger, and then he calmly asked, "Anything else you want to tell me?"

Dr. Dravinski didn't want to tell Reynolds about his suspicions or the plan he was brewing up in his mind. It was only necessary to him that Reynolds pull back and give him enough time to put things in motion on his end. It would be the only way he could prove his hypothesis.

"Sec. Reynolds, just give me at least forty-eight hours. That's all I need. I feel I'm onto something!"

He waited for an answer, but there was none, just breathing on the other end. Finally, Reynolds spoke, "There's obviously something that you're unwilling to share with me, and I must tell you that I'm deeply offended." Then Dravinski heard that famous Reynolds chuckle coming through the phone, "Walter, Walter, Walter, May I call you Walter, old friend? Okay, forty-eight hours. You play the game your way; I'll play the game my way. Two traps are better than one, good day!" And with that, the line went dead.

Dr. Dravinski realized his boss was losing it, or maybe he was always insane. He looked at his watch and realized that it would be another hour or two before Colonel Novak landed in Addis Ababa. He couldn't waste any more time; he needed to go through some notes, any leads Dr. Eleazar might have left behind in her Paris office. Just as he was leaving the airport restaurant, he saw a few PT97s a distance away. Are they watching me too? He wondered.

If nothing else he knew Reynolds was, he had to play it carefully, for there was too much at stake. When he would get to his hotel, he would change his registration and go to another hotel – just in case. This was not a good time to become paranoid, but Dr. Dravinski knew the game too well. Just because Reynolds offered to back off didn't mean he would slack off on his surveillance.

# 8

Dr. Dravinski was in Dr. Eleazar's Paris office, going through whatever he could get his hands on, searching for any clues leading to where she might have gone or what she was up to. Dravinski went about high-jacking two computers in her office with a viral inscription, re-starter virus, but came up with nothing. It didn't help his investigation to realize that he was still some days behind Dr. Eleazar.

He sat in her office chair and ransacked through her desk draws. He leaned back in the chair and tried to think of what she would do, how her mind worked. He thought about when he knew her and worked with her four years earlier at Artificial Universe Corporation. He had grown fond of her, admiring her intellect and her lovely sense of humor that added to her beauty. They worked on augmenting nanotechnology solutions, and he looked forward to establishing a relationship with her. That was before his transfer to the position he holds now, once news of his status as a young officer in the First Corporation Conflict came to light.

He realized that nothing in her office offered any info about her whereabouts.

He got up from her seat and did his best to rearrange a portion of the mess he had created as a few eyes of her corporate colleagues questioned his being there, even though he had his corporation badge attached to his lapel.

When he got back to his hotel, he called Colonel Novak.

"Dr. Dravinski, how are you? I've been waiting for your call here in Addis Ababa. I've been here with my team for about an hour or so. Now, what is it that you have in mind? I hope it is something worthwhile."

He could tell Col. Novak was somewhat irritated with him, but it was the least of his concerns.

"Well, while I'm telling you this," one could hear the caution in his voice, "My phone, along with yours, in fact, this entire conversation is probably being monitored by Sec. Reynolds or 'Mother.'"

"Sec. Reynolds, I can understand, but 'Mother?' What are you implying?"

"My view? I think something is wrong with Mother, and whatever it is, it's affecting a few selected droids out of the millions manufactured the world over. To what scale, I have no idea, from a handful to maybe a hundred or so, but something is happening," Dr. Dravinski explained.

"Can you prove it? How can you be sure? That's a little too far-fetched for me to believe."

"I can't quite prove it, can't quite get a handle on it yet, which is why I sent you to Addis Ababa, along with some other units, to different locations in Eastern Europe. I feel that there's something else going on, and psychics are an essential piece of the puzzle.

"Corporations and governments are too quick to erase a problem than discover if there really is a problem in the first place. Empaths may not be getting corporate or government secrets. We may have been killing empaths for all the wrong reasons. We need to capture some and hold them so that our monitors can get a closer look at what's going on. I mean, it's all just a theory, but it's been bugging me in the back of my mind for quite some time now."

"Is that why you had me bring the PT97s along?" Col. Novak asked.

"Yes, but keep them hidden from sight, in a closed, concealed van or truck. Make friends with the locals of a small village or city and locate their shamans and upon capturing one or two, bring them near the droids. Now, remember to keep the droids from public view."

"You're right about one thing, doctor; most empaths move out of the way of droids. In fact, many of them have even been known to leave or flee towns and villages that PT97s have patrolled. I guess, over the years, the rumors or truths of what we have done to sensitives have gotten out," the colonel added.

"Let me know when you have completed your mission. We got less than forty-eight hours. I'll coordinate the data from the other groups and see what we can find out or get an idea of what is going on. Remember, our conversation is probably already being recorded and reviewed. So, we'll talk later."

"Yes sir, later it is," Col. Novak said, turning off the scrambler on his end. He always employed a scrambler. Reynolds may be listening, but it will take them some time to decipher their conversation. He had only hoped the other units used scramblers as well. After all, for the most part, it was protocol, but then again, he knew too many sloppy corporate people.

# 9

Sec. Reynolds sat in his office chair and puffed on his AniverXario cigar. He pushed a few items around on his desk, aligned some pencils and fountain pens in order, shuffled some papers, and thought about his conversation with Dr. Dravinski. And then mentally shoved the discussion to the side like one of the other objects on his desk.

After a few more puffs, he picked up a secured phone line and decided to bring in The Spaniard, one of his most notorious covert operatives. He waited and listened as someone picked up the other end, "Mr. Cortez, good afternoon. I was hoping you could come to my home office ASAP. I want you by my side to listen to a communique briefing with Dr. Dravinski, who is currently in Paris. I just sent you a PDF file for viewing concerning some of his latest communique with Colonel Novak."

"Mr. Secretary, I'm on my way, sir. Oh, by the way, I heard about the excursions in Eastern Europe, sorry I couldn't have been there; I could've used the trip," responded the smooth, polished, Spanish accented voice of Mr. Cortez.

"Not to worry, Mr. Cortez, I'll have several things lined up for you very shortly."

"I'm at your bidding, as always, sir. It's a pleasure working with you," he said, hanging up the phone and looking to check the PDF file Reynolds sent.

After reviewing the file and making a few mental notes, he placed his phone on his dresser and proceeded to tie his tie in a four-in-hand knot, finishing with handsome cufflinks. He holstered his semi-automatic pistol and put on a finely tailored suit jacket. He ordered his transportation on his phone and, as he headed out, stopped to pose his tall, manly frame, looking long enough in the full-length mirror by the door to make sure his hair, neatly combed and thin mustache well-groomed. He placed on his well-tailored Fedora and angled it just so; he had to admit he liked what he saw. He always had a flair for being well-dressed.

When he reached the lobby of his hotel and stepped out of the elevator, he quickly reacted to catch a tossed ball from a four-year child playing by the bank of elevators. He returned it to her and patted her on the head, leaving her mother to admire this dashing Spaniard. He gave her a courteous bow with a slight tip of his hat and headed toward the entrance, motioning to his men, Nelson and Hunter, who were waiting in the hotel lobby, to accompany him. They quickly rose and were at his side.

He was a polished man who tolerated little; still, he was patient, courteous, and well-mannered in his behavior with most people as a whole, unless, of course, you happen to fall in the crosshairs of a business contract.

Colonel Novak looked at his timepiece, being that it was an hour earlier in Paris and after breakfast, he figured it would be a good enough time to call, so he got on the phone with Dr. Dravinski, telling him that he was able to sneak into a village at dawn before anyone had awakened. Novak said to him that he was able to hire a woman from a neighboring town to pretend she required the need of the local shaman.

When she learned where she could find him, she went to his house. Col. Novak followed her to the location and broke in on him. The team restrained him from escaping custody, bringing him to meet the PT97s.

"It was astonishing," Col. Novak said. "When we brought him close to the PT97s, he just collapsed to the ground. Our monitors had to carry him to a nearby house.

"It took several attempts to find the correct distance between him and the droids. You know, the range that would allow him to be awake and yet still under the influence of the droids.

"I waited until our team injected him with sodium pentothal (truth serum), and when he was under, we asked him about what was he experiencing.

"He said that he was receiving images from the PT97 androids, but these PT97s themselves were unaware of receiving any images

"He said that of the many visions he saw in his mind, there was one of a strange land he had never been to, possibly another country. He kept seeing the number thirty-seven, a crater in a desert region; a sign in what he thought was English, but he couldn't read it, just kept seeing an image of the corners of four squares coming together over and over again. He finally said two rivers were joining together, and he thought he saw the pyramids of Cairo, but he knew it wasn't Cairo, just the same name.

"What do you think it means, Dr. Dravinski?" Col. Novak asked him.

"It's only an initial confirmation, but I think on some level Mother is developing a level of consciousness that is affecting particular androids in the system, and it's such that clairvoyants and sensitives are affected by it." Dr. Dravinski went on, "I'm just waiting to gather similar information from some other groups I have in Eastern Europe. When I do, I'll be able to present my conclusions to the home office. I should be hearing them in about—"

Suddenly, their communique broke – static, almost shattering their eardrums. They heard a voice breaking through, screaming at both of them. "Turn it off! Turn it off!" Turn off that damn scrambler, Col. Novak! That's an order!"

It was Sec. Reynolds, hacking their phone line. Upon recognizing his voice, Colonel Novak immediately switched off the scrambler device.

"Interesting conversation the both of you have been having. I must say, Dr. Dravinski, I like the way your analytical mind operates," Sec. Reynolds said while nodding to Mr. Cortez sitting across from him.

"I was just following a hunch, nothing more. I didn't want to tell you anything until I could confirm my suspicions. I'm still waiting for other calls from—" Dravinski said.

"Forget it. That won't be necessary. This is good enough info to go on." Reynolds said, cutting him off.

"Still, sir, I would personally feel better with more confirmations."

"Dr. Dravinski, in no way am I stopping you from receiving your necessary communications. You can continue doing what it was you were doing before I interrupted you, but as far as I'm concerned, it's good enough for me to proceed on my end."

Dr. Dravinski didn't like Reynolds's smooth, calculating tone. He was getting somewhat agitated with his superior. As it was, he was highly infuriated with Reynolds breaking in on his communique with Col. Novak the way he did, barking orders like some mad dog. He thought he would back off and give him some space; still, in truth, he knew better than that. He just swallowed and ended the conversation with, "Yes, sir."

Reynolds took a well-smoked cigar out of his mouth and pressed his intercom bracelet, and then spoke to his technical staff. "This is Sec. Reynolds, I just wanted to compliment you and your techs for doing a fine job de-scrambling the earlier communique between Dr. Dravinski and Col. Novak and helping us break through his current communique. Extend my compliments to your team."

"Thank you, sir, will do," a voice responded over the com-bracelet.

"One more thing," Reynolds continued, "how is our stockpile in Hangar #23?"

"Well, over a thousand, sir. Will that be all?"

"Yes, thank you," Sec. Reynolds answered him, putting down the phone.

Sec. Reynolds picked up the remains of his cigar and found a comfortable niche for it in his mouth. He got up and paced his office with a wicked smile, stopping by to pat Mr. Cortez on his shoulder and strolled over to the picture of the banned GT84s and, referring to them, said, "It looks like there's going to be room for you guys to get back in the game after all."

He just stood there and chuckled to himself.


Sec. Reynolds returned to his desk, pulled out his revolver, and holstered it. He picked up his phone and made a call to the Director of Robotic Analysis at Area 51. "Director Andrews, this is Secretary Reynolds. Please meet me at Hangar #23 in Area 51. Oh, am I right in assuming the portable Hub for the GT84s is still operational?"

"Yes, sir."

"Good, fire it up. I'll be boarding a slider from D.C., be there shortly, and please keep this as confidential as possible. It is on a need-to-know basis."

"Yes, sir, expecting you shortly."

He looked at Cortez, who was already making calls to have his team meet them at Area 51.

"I like the way you think, Cortez," Reynolds said.

"It's in the blood, sir," he answered and gestured an assuring nod to the Secretary of State and then notified his limousine driver that they were coming outside for a ride to the airport.

# 10

Dr. Eleazar walked the streets of Paris, picking up a few things for supper. They had been in Paris a few days before Dr. Dravinski had arrived. Malcolm accompanied her as they walked. He was wearing corporate security markings and had holstered "Disabler" on his right hip.

Disablers were precisely what the name implied, similar to the earlier century-old tasers. They would only disable the target. Projected prongs fired from a disabler would get an instantaneous readout from the weapon's targeting array, identifying the target as flesh, metal, or plastic base or combination, and it would instantly apply a predesignated electrical charge to bring down or disable the mark in question.

A postal package was delivered to Dr. Eleazar's hotel room a few hours after they arrived with two corporate security emblems and two disablers, so they decided to put them on. While she was in Paris, she decided to continue wearing a simple headscarf to reduce the risk of any facial recognition devices.

As Malcolm and Dr. Eleazar approached the entrance to their hotel, they saw Solomon talking with the android doorman. He saw them coming and acknowledged them with a casual nod. The three of them entered the building together as Dr. Eleazar held a curious gaze on Solomon, the kind to make him turn toward her as they walked into the elevator, and so he asked her, "Is there something wrong?"

"I was just wondering," she questioned, looking for the right words to phrase her question, "Can droids, who are dreamers, recognize other dreamers, the way humans can tell or guess by looks where a fellow countryman, stranger, or foreigner might come from?"

"Yes, we can also recognize the factory origin of another android, but in case you're wondering, our doorman is a dreamer. He told me you rarely ever come here."

"That's true. This isn't my real apartment in Paris; I actually live in a more expensive, upper-class district. I come here once in a blue moon. Like when I'm trying to get away from it all, the press and the interviews. I come here when I don't want to be found or just when I need time to think or work on solving problems; virtually no one knows about his place."

"Well, considering we got that postal package, someone is keeping tabs on you."

"Maybe the doorman got the word out to other dreamers." She added.

"There are probably a few other dreamers in here, for I know the others in our team now have this location."

"Okay, that's good." She concluded as the elevator doors opened.

They got off on the seventh floor and entered the small but well-kept suite. She placed a few shopping bags on the table and sat on the chair across from Solomon, and began nervously looking through some hotel magazines on the coffee table. She found herself turning page after page, not reading, not even reading – just turning

Malcolm came into the room and noticed her fidgeting with the magazines, "Withdrawal, eh?"

"What?"

"How long have you been without an electronic device in your hand, more than twenty-four hours? I'm surprised you've lasted *this* long."

She plopped the magazines down and started a quiet giggle that grew louder. She regained control and wiped her eyes that had begun to tear. "Perceptive, aren't we? But, you're right. Wow! I certainly didn't realize I had it so bad, but there it is. I need to touch a keyboard, phone, or some kind of device I can piggyback my thoughts on to, so I can slip through time unnoticed. In truth, I'm worried about the guys; I hope they're doing well."

Malcolm looked over to Solomon; they both understood what she meant, and while they knew the definitive meaning of the word, the concept of "worry" was still new to them.

"You know," she added, "I feel bad about not contacting my brother Matthew or Aster, my sister. I mean, let's face it, I kind of left my brother in the dark with just that one message that I was needed back at work. I'm sure Matthew and Aster have been trying to reach me, but for their own safety and mine, I feel it's for the best they don't know."

"Is your family close?" Malcolm figured it'd be a good idea to converse with her.

She leaned back in the chair, reminiscing, "My family is not as close as I'd like us to be, now that we're older. Matthew was always there for me whenever I needed him when we were kids. However, when my parents got the chance to come to the United States, he didn't want to travel here.

"In the beginning, he was rebellious and had a rough time in the school system. I guess the idea of me being a 'child star' was hard on him, with him being the firstborn and only male child.

"Unfortunately for him and Aster, I was always in the zone, in my world of custom robotic designs and formulations, pretty much my haven of wonder.

"Matthew found his way through. Yeah, Matthew found his way," she repeated in deep thought. "He created his own business, Promised Land Real Estate, and sold real estate in the U.S. and the world over. It seemed that once he established his footing, our relationship improved.

"Aster, on the other hand, was more like me, only her skill was in the field of commercial and graphic art. In fact, some of the outfitting for many androids comes from her designs. She's a sharp, beautiful woman married to a fine man, Daniel."

She stood up from the chair; tears were gathering in her eyes.

Malcolm presumed it would be a good time to change the subject, "Do you want me to activate the viewing screen?"

"You can turn it on; just leave the volume off. I need to go into the kitchen and fix myself something to eat."

Malcolm and Solomon watched her as she walked into the dinette area. Solomon carried her bags into the bedroom. No one saw the French newscast with words flashing across the screen: "LIGHTS OVER CAIRO!" — Along with a brief video of unknown crafts skirting across the night sky.

# 11

Sec. Reynolds and Mr. Cortez were about five minutes from Area 51 when the monitor on the Secretary's slider began broadcasting news reports about lights over the city of Cairo, Illinois. Reynolds and Cortez walked over to the monitor, turning up the volume.

"Initially rumored, it now has been confirmed, by several eyewitnesses, a group of unidentified crafts was seen in the night sky over the city of Cairo, Illinois, along the western riverbank this evening." Sec. Reynolds immediately called his investigative tech team in Washington, D.C., to see if the report correlated with images currently being deciphered from the Ethiopian shaman's vision. Now that Reynolds heard this report about possible UFOs over Cairo, he wanted confirmation.

While confirming with his tech, Mr. Cortez notified a corporate squad in the mid-states to prepare for an immediate airlift. He told the party on the other end to hold the line while he waited for a cue from Reynolds.

"You say the number thirty-seven appears to refer to the thirty-seventh parallel, and the four square coming together can only mean one thing – four corners? That's excellent!" He said, motioning to Mr. Cortez, "Keep me updated!"

"Take a squad on an HH 80G PAVE Hawk helicopter to Four Corners monument," Cortez continued with his phone contact. He nodded back to Reynolds, confirming everything. He and Reynolds put down their phones to watch the rest of the broadcast. The announcer told everyone not to worry because they dispatched a unit of PT97s to investigate the sighting and possible landing area.

Cortez looked at Reynolds, confused, "Sir, I don't recall you sending any PT97s to investigate anything?"

"I didn't," he said.

"Then who did?"

"Mother!" Sec. Reynolds cringed. Cortez could hear Reynolds' teeth grinding together.

"Please, fasten your seat belts. We will be landing at Area 51 shortly," the pilot voiced over the loudspeakers, accompanied by flashing lights. Cortez worked his phone as they were landing to activate units in the area.

Base officials greeted them, and Director Andrews drove them to Hangar #23, followed by a few other vehicles with Cortez's men who had landed at the heliport earlier. Area 51 had grown relatively larger in the past two hundred years.

"Sir, may I ask why the need to activate the AI Hub for the GT84s?" Dir. Andrews asked Sec. Reynolds while walking on the way over.

"Situation protocol keeps me from revealing any information. The reason for our presence at this facility is on a need-to-know basis. Should the parameters change, you will be informed accordingly."

Director Andrews nodded dutifully.

When they arrived, they came into the hangar with its frontal row of lights on with the AI Hub located on a small, central platform in front of row upon row of GT84s extending far back in the hangar.

One of Cortez's men flipped on the ceiling lights, and there were over a thousand droids in the hangar.

Dir. Andrews tugged lightly on Reynolds' arm, pointing out the colored zones painted on the hangar's concrete floor. "From what we have accessed, based on our studies, we've placed those GT84s with the least neural damage in the blue zone, while those in the dark red zones toward the back are the most unstable."

Andrews acquainted Reynolds and Cortez with the controls on the Hub as they related to the zoned androids and their activation.

Cortez told Andrews to activate twenty GT84s in the blue zone. Andrews looked toward Sec. Reynolds, hoping for confirmation. Reynolds nodded.

"Have ten board each one of the transport helicopters outside the hangar."

Andrews turned with a worried face to Cortez, then quickly looked for further confirmation from Sec. Reynolds then went to a shelf containing columns and rows of audio control helmets behind him. He selected one and imputed the ID codes of the twenty chosen droids. He handed the helm to Cortez to wear to maintain control over the droids in the field.

Cortez placed it on his head, activated it, and told the droids to advance. A group of twenty droids did so,

71

and he ordered them into two groups of ten and had them refitted with weaponry, and then ordered them to board the two transport helicopters standing outside the hangar. Cortez had yet to depart as he waited for a signal from Sec. Reynolds.

After a few minutes, Sec. Reynolds' phone began to ring. He repeated what was said to him so that Cortez could hear it. "The crater is the Uberhebe Crater in Death Valley, the small crater next to it, called Little Hebe. Unidentified crafts have been spotted heading in that direction."

Mr. Cortez gave him a thumbs-up salute and ran to join his squad and the others, leaving three members of his unit to remain with Sec. Reynolds, Dir. Andrews and a few base security personnel.

Sec. Reynolds ended his phone call just in time to see the helicopters lift off.

# 12

Dr. Eleazar, Solomon, and Malcolm were rushing home through the crowded streets of Paris, walking at a good pace without trying to draw too much attention. There was a broadcast on a news station airing on a billboard on a building in Paris about a TEDS Scoop trying to cross the Atlantic Ocean and had either crashed or was blown out of the sky by Tracker Drones. She maintained her headscarf as she hurried along the streets.

As they approached their hotel, the doorman droid motioned to Solomon and briefly coded with him, telling them they had guests upstairs.

As they rode the elevator up, Dr. Eleazar could feel her nerve endings tingle in heightened anxiety.

When they walked into the suite, they saw Angola, Estcban, and Elijah coding as if going over the details of their missions.

"Where's Samson?" Dr. Eleazar immediately asked she knew by the way Elijah held himself that something was wrong, "What happened to Samson?"

Malcolm tried to reassure her with a soothing, "Let them tell their story, Yohanna." He thought using her first name might help make the request easier. He could see where this was going if things didn't calm down.

Solomon stepped in and said to them, "Let's do this by order of assignment, as we're supposed to be doing before we lose our heads and go off the deep end. Angola report!"

Everyone quieted down and looked at Angola.

"My mission went rather smoothly, even though I was prepared should things get out of hand. Instead, when my Scoop pilot Andre landed near a water treatment plant outside of Cairo, Illinois, we were met by six PT97s armed with Disablers. They had already put two human security monitors to sleep with gas. They gave me the rod, and I put it in my chest case. Then Andre scooped me to Chicago's International Airport to wait for the others."

He opened a chest plate, took out the rod, and showed them when he finished. It looked as Yohanna had said.

Solomon nodded, "Esteban report!"

"My assignment was pretty much like Angola's. At first, it went smoothly. It was dark, and there was no one in sight, except after the group of six droids met us. We were about to hand over the rod when a squad of corporate covert ops, who must have been masking their heat signatures, opened fire on us with phaser rifles and automatic weapons.

"Two of the droids, who met us, went down immediately. I activated my shielding, which helped. We fired our Disablers, but they wore insulated armor. Fortunately, two of the droids who met us were upgraded, crowd-control gas droids. That caught our attackers by surprise. Kronos, my pilot, and the rest of us set our weapons to the max and tripled up on our Disablers shots. In the chaos, with the gas and firings, they went down.

"The two gas droids were too severely injured, and Kronos had to use a 'Wiper' on them to erase their memory along with the other two damaged droids.

"Kronos took me to O'Hare International as well to meet up with Angola and wait."

He took out his rod from his chest-case pocket and showed it to Solomon and the others.

They all turned to Eli; they prepared to hear a harrowing story. Still, all they could do was wait for what was to come. Solomon didn't have to ask Eli to report; he just began.

"When Orion took Samson and me in along Little Hebe's rim, and we were about to land, two transport helicopters came in firing on the two teams of PT97s who quickly looked for cover and started shooting back.

"Samson and I were already sitting on our packing crates in the back of the Scoop. Having passed inspection at our last stop, Orion took us down low to the ground and told us to jump. Samson and I had our Pulse rifle and Disabler.

"When we landed, we took cover like our brothers and fired at the transports. Orion took his Scoop to a higher altitude and fired his Disabler over and over again at the turrets. The helicopters came down hard, injuring some ops, but when they landed, the remaining squad and about twenty GT84s came out of the downed choppers, firing pulse and automatic weapons."

He paused and looked at Dr. Eleazar and realized the look of dismay she held in her face.

"We were about a hundred meters away from a tourist/ ranger station and a recently constructed overnight hotel. There were tourists inside, not many but enough for us to be concerned about them.

"As the GT84s advanced toward us, a number of the PT97s worked their way into the station. They warned

75

the tourists and personnel and helped them evacuate. We were fortunate that the three rangers on duty recognized the GT84s and, knowing their history, picked up their weapons and started firing on them.

"With the corporate covert squad and the GT84s, we were outnumbered two to one; without hesitation, one of our brothers rolled to a point just passed the GT84s and released its gas as both ops and droids shot everything they had at him. But his effort wasn't in vain; I could see the humans going down with one last human who wore a helmet still standing, firing at Orion in the scoop. He was the last to go down. I think he must have been the one giving the GT84s their orders.

"I don't know what he told them, but whatever it was, they went into a crazed frenzy, putting out so much firepower that the tower at the ranger station began to crumble under the weight of repeated gunfire. When the humans were out of the picture, Samson raised both phase rifle and Disabler, and he was brutally effective with every shot he made.

"I, on the other hand, still couldn't bring myself to fire on another droid. The most I could do was shoot at support structures as they drove us further into the building. I did my best to slow them down as much as possible. Once inside the building, the PT97s who still had our rods passed them to us. For a brief moment, it appeared we actually might be able to hold out on our own.

"Orion was above them still firing, and somehow he continued to avoid their return fire.

"We neared the exit doors on the other side of the building when three GT84s charged ahead, weapons blazing suddenly. Samson fell right next to me, virtually cut in half. More brothers came to our aide, throwing themselves in front of us to keep us from getting shot. Their bodies piled up in front of me. I fired blindly, not knowing who or what I was hitting.

"Suddenly, I felt something grab my leg like a vice. It was Samson yelling at me, 'Get the hell out of here now!' and then he said, 'Dream on, good brother!'

"I knew what he meant when he said that he was going to self-destruct. I saw Orion land his scoop outside the exit doors, and I ran for it. I scrambled onto the scoop as it lifted off with Orion firing at the oncoming 84s, and then the whole building went up in a massive fireball that tore it and everything around it apart. Samson took himself out and every other droid in the complex. I can only hope that some of the innocent humans got away safely.

"As I climbed in the scoop, I realized that there was some kind of tracking device implanted near the backside of the scoop. Probably put there by the human wearing the helmet.

"I told Orion about it as he was climbing to gain altitude, but he said that it was the least of his concerns. He had to get me to Chicago airport.

"I could see that he was damaged, I asked him if there was anything I could do, but he never answered me. Once we landed in Chicago, he told me to get out and go to the slider. I stood by him, making sure he was okay. He coded with another droid after refueling his scoop. The droid climbed in, and I was about to pull the tracking device when he told me to leave it in."

"'Listen,' he told me, 'they're tracking two droids in a scoop. I'll draw them off; you join Esteban and Angola. Dream on!'

"With that, he lifted off to an altitude far too high for a scoop. It was as if he was treating his craft like a slider, as if he was trying to reach the East Coast or Europe. I saw him take off, and when I reached the slider, I turned to look up and saw two tracker-attack drones climbing in altitude to following his route."

After Elijah finished, he stood there, unable to move an inch; he didn't even realize that he had been telling them his tale with his head bent down all the while. He slowly raised his head to see tears running down the face of Dr. Eleazar.

Seeing her, he offered his sentiment, "I wish we could express that emotion. I truly do." He opened his sorely battered chest plate and showed Solomon the rod given to him.

Solomon saw it but stepped back, expecting to see two of them, "Where is the device given to Samson?"

"I don't know; he never had the chance to pass it to me."

"What?" Solomon's voice expressed an extraordinary level of concern not heard by the others before. He turned as if needing a moment to reflect on what to do.

"How can we do this without the fourth rod?" Malcolm exclaimed.

"We do what we must; we go onto the next level. One way or another, we'll figure this out; we'll find a way," said Dr. Eleazar, drying her eyes and walking across to pour herself a small glass of wine. She looked at all five of them, tears still streaming down her cheeks, raised her glass, and emptied a small amount of the wine on the floor. In a shaky heartfelt voice, she offered libation, "To Samson, his spirit, his strength, his sacrifice. Dream on." She drank the rest and sat on a stool with her head down.

# 13

Mr. Cortez was quite dazed when he finally awoke. The Ranger Station was smoldering and still partly in flames as the night sky was beginning to reveal the coming of dawn in the distance. He caught sight of Hunter and Nelson and some other team members slowly recovering along with him. Only five of them survived the firefight with the Rangers from the tower outside of himself.

Cortez ordered the team to search for any survivors and take care of them accordingly when they could regain their senses. He told them to look through the debris for anything unusual or out of the ordinary. Of course, they would have to check for anyone at the hotel as no calls should've gotten out, considering they placed a low-level dampening field on the area before they came in, enough to disrupt radio and phone transmissions.

After some time, he hotwired an abandoned car and slowly drove it down the road for about a mile to get out of the dissipating dampening zone. Stopped, got out, and checked to see if his cell phone was working. He called Sec. Reynolds. Told him that his team was securing the area. However, they were unable to find anything out of the norm yet. Cortez told him how the PT97s had fared well enough just to survive the attack by his team and the GT84s.

"Another strange thing, sir," Mr. Cortez continued.

"What?"

"From the damage, there seems to have been a central, massive explosion of some sort. I think one of the PT97s self-detonated."

"Not possible, never heard of such a thing!"

"With all due respect, sir, unless it was an airstrike of some kind which I strongly doubt, it certainly appears that way."

"Okay," said Reynolds, "I'll send in a cleanup crew. We can keep this out of the media for only a few days under the guise of national defense protocols and spin it to discredit any survivors, but a few days is all we should need to wrap this mess up. By then, we'll come up with a convincing cover story. Were there any witnesses?"

"None that I am currently aware of; they would've had to walk out of here. My crew is mopping up, sir."

"Good. Mr. Cortez, I'm sending you a chopper as we speak. I need you in New York City ASAP. Have some members of your New York team meet you there. I'll email you a PDF with target specifics.

"I wanted you to know that we did send two tracker-attack drones after the scoop that left your area after it rose above the dampening field. Nice idea to put a tracking device on it just in case things went sour."

"Did you take it down?"

"Yes, we did," Sec. Reynolds added, "that fool of a pilot must've thought he was flying a slider. He refueled at O'Hare International Airport, took off way above restricted altitude for a scoop, and tried to make it across the Atlantic Ocean. He must've been damaged to the point where his logic-processing systems malfunctioned. The cameras on our drones showed it was one hell of a wild ride before they took him down over the ocean, but we got him in the long run. He was lucky to get as far as he did."

"Very good, sir, and please accept my apologies for this mishap."

"Not to worry, sometimes the mouse slips out of the trap. It's what makes the game a game. Otherwise, there'd be nothing to enjoy."

"Okay, I need to contact my New York team, as I'm sure you need to contact yours."

"Yes, my tech crew is going over Dr. Eleazar's surveillance tapes with a fine-tooth comb. I'll get back with you should anything come up."

"Thank you, sir," Cortez hung up, but there was still an inkling of dissatisfaction that was bothering him.

Mr. Cortez stood there in a quiet rage, and he paced around the car. Several times he kicked at the tires. The Spaniard was the type of man who didn't tolerate failure or dealing with being outmaneuvered like in the incident a few hours earlier. Cortez decided to calm down and focus on what he needed to do next. He checked the email file Reynolds sent him. It displayed Dr. Eleazar's brother, Matthew, and instructions.

He would have Nelson and Hunter go with him, and then he put in some calls.

Later in the evening of the next day at the 20th Precinct at 82nd street in New York, Matthew, Yohanna's brother, was in a small office sweating the questions hurled at him. He was extremely nervous, yet still confident, for in truth, he had no idea where his sister was or even why he was in for interrogation a second time.

The attitude of one of the corporate agents questioning him became increasingly more hostile and more violent towards him as the grilling continued. The detective began striking him with a few vicious blows to the head and face, along with the socially unacceptable use of some race-baiting words being injected now and then during the interrogation.

Sec. Reynolds watched the whole live-stream interrogation process unfold on his lap monitor in a darkened corner of Hangar #23 away from the remaining personnel. There was just enough light to highlight the shape of his hard, grim face. He was highly displeased with what he saw and the sloppy way they handled it, snapping a group of pencils in half in the left hand as he tensed up. He leaned forward, picked his phone on the desk, and put in a call to New York.

Looking at his watch and realizing the questioning had been going on for nearly three hours. He waited as the phone on the other end rang. Finally, someone in the office answered; all they heard was a crude, dry voice slowly saying, "Tell them to close it down and let Matthew go."

The agent recognized the phone ID.

Reynolds knew Cortez was already in New York waiting outside the 20th Precinct.

The door to the interrogation room opened, and an agent said, "We have orders to release him."

The two agents looked surprised, if not disappointed, knowing there was no point in disagreeing with the order. One of the agents who questioned him gave him a condescending grin and offered Matthew some medication to cover the worst of his bruises. He slapped the agent's hand away, "No thanks, I need to remember this!" He left the room with both men satisfied with themselves and their actions.

Angry but glad to get the hell out of there, Matthew took a long, fuming walk down the Westside. When he reached 75th Street, he was still livid with what he had undergone. Matthew wondered what his sister had gotten herself involved with and if she was okay. He decided to stop and enter a vegetable store to pick up a few things before going up to his apartment.

A black sedan that had been trailing him pulled over, and two hooded men, Cortez and Nelson, calmly slipped out of the vehicle and proceeded to walk to where Matthew stood, placing red peppers into a bag.

Mr. Cortez tapped Matthew on his shoulder and said, "Sir, I believe this is yours."

Matthew turned to see a revolver with a silencer facing him as two slugs slammed into his skull. He crumbled to the sidewalk with people screaming all around him.

Nelson, Cortez's backup, came up from behind him, yelling at Matthew's body, "There's more of this for the rest of your family!" He put one more slug into Matthew's lifeless body. Cortez even had another member of his hit team filming it from across the street so that an anonymous video would suddenly appear on a broadcast anchor's news desk.

The two shooters climbed back into the car as it sped off into the night, leaving people screaming, others taking videos and pictures of Matthew's body lying in the street.

At the same time, the store manager called for the police and emergency unit.

Mr. Cortez pulled off his hood and calmly texted Sec as the car sped south. Reynolds two letters – DD (code for "Done Deal").

*Yes, it should make tomorrow's front-page news;* Sec. Reynolds chuckled to himself, looking at the message on his phone that he pulled from his vest pocket. He made a text to Mr. Cortez to keep his team on hold and await further instructions. A slim, wicked smile came to the surface of his darkened face, "Okay, Dr. Dravinski," he told himself, "Your turn."

# 14

Dr. Eleazar picked up one of her pads and pens that Malcolm had provided her with; she felt the need to write, to put something down on paper, thoughts, emotions, anything. She feared the journey they were on might not succeed, even after the speech she had given earlier. In truth, they didn't have all the pieces to the puzzle. She was also concerned about the activation and introduction of the GT84s and who was behind it all.

The suite had grown crowded with five androids and one human. Elijah had been quiet ever since he gave his report. He wasn't the same. Samson's termination affected him more than the others would've predicted. He might be suffering from survivor's guilt and feeling responsible for Samson's death, owing to his lack of lethal action against the GT84s.

Dr. Eleazar remembered some of the work she was involved with as a consultant to a team studying the effects of PTSD on the GT84s. She could sense a change in Elijah. She knew all the others were either concerned about his state, thinking of Samson, or held doubts about completing the mission.

She sat on a high chair in a peaceful, quiet corner of the kitchen, putting thoughts to paper. Malcolm worked his way over to where she sat and asked, "Madam, can I make you some tea?"

She looked up at him. "Oh, no, thank you, Malcolm, but thanks."

He was about to turn away when she touched his arm, "Malcolm," and asked quietly, "is it true that dreamers can self-terminate like Samson, Orion, and the droid who was with him. Are you capable of sacrificing yourself?"

Malcolm stood still and, in a quiet voice, said, "I don't know if it is an actual sacrifice as humans would call it or simply the most logical course of action one can make that would benefit the outcome for all involved in an attempt to achieve a specific outcome."

"Then I guess it is an act both droids and humans often make," she offered a smile of thanks to Malcolm when suddenly everyone in the suite could feel the wave. It felt like it could've gone through the whole floor of the building.

The droids looked at each other and then looked at her, "It's a trail we need to follow in the Himalayan mountain range, again along or near the thirty-seventh parallel. We'll need to take a sky-slider to Lhasa, Tibet, in China, and from there go to a site on or near Mt. Kailash."

She looked worried, realizing she had no electronic devices to make any of the arrangements she needed to make. Suddenly there was a knock on the door. Solomon went to check on who it was.

It was one of the maintenance droids. It coded with Solomon for a few seconds; he returned with a package having everyone's arrangements. It held the TEDS slider tickets for crate shipment for Esteban, Angola, and Elijah; it also had slider tickets for Dr. Eleazar, Solomon, and Malcolm.

"Okay, let's wrap it up." Malcolm was eager to leave.

While they were all in the room, Solomon went over to Elijah and put his hand on his shoulder, "Brother, are you going to be alright? You've experienced something the rest of us have yet to experience. Still, I need to hear it from you."

Elijah looked at Solomon and the rest of them and said, "It's something Samson would expect of me, no matter what, it's something I'm willing to do to honor his sacrifice and memory. One way or another, I offer you guys the best I have to offer.'

It was enough for them to hear. Dr. Eleazar went to her room and started packing.

# 15

Dr. Dravinski received a coded message on his laptop. He opened it to see a news report showing Dr. Eleazar's brother, Matthew lying dead on the streets of New York with images of people screaming and some footage of the incident from across the street showing the killers in action.

He logged onto his laptop for a video conference. He had known Matthew and was visibly upset that things could have gone this far. Quickly, he gathered his senses together; he answered, "Yes, yes, I'm here. Sir, sometimes I just don't understand why you even think you can get results doing what you do. What the hell were you thinking by killing Dr. Eleazar's brother, Matthew?"

"Got you upset, did it now?" he said with a gleeful undertone. "Good, good! Very good! We're hoping and expecting it to have the same effect on Dr. Eleazar. Now maybe that little rebellious twit will stop her ridiculous games and come out of hiding to warn her younger sister. We can then monitor the call and locate her whereabouts!"

"With all due respect, sir, that's not her profile. She's much too smart to fall for an obvious trap!" he tried to sound like he was offering him sound advice, when in truth, the few memories he held of Matthew was that of a handsome young man with his promising career, kept clouding his thoughts.

"I can hear the sympathy and regret in your voice, Walter. What, did you know him? Well, it's not for me to concern myself with the opinions of bleeding hearts that hold no weight, no depth of influence like yourself. It's just another reason why you'll never rise to a position of effective power and authority. You keep seeing tragedy in the lost pawns when I'm after the queen. Now, do you have any other opinions or words of wisdom you wish to pass on to me?"

"No sir," Dr. Dravinski said, closing his laptop hearing the closing words of Reynolds, "I didn't think so."

Dr. Dravinski went over to the bar in his hotel suite and poured himself a drink while he strolled over to the window and looked out on the beautiful city of Paris. He was a well-educated man, well aware of harsh truths in government or corporate politics as it was made more apparent to him today. World governments were merely fronts for corporate empires; puppet rulers controlled by puppeteers who orchestrated Life's operas on a world stage, He and Sec. Reynolds was the corporate stagehands that worked the curtains and stage devices that changed the scenery. They turned day into night in the lives of small people like Matthew and soon-to-be Yohanna, who he had come to care for in the few years he'd known her.

For a moment, he wished he was somewhere else, maybe even somebody else. Then he finished his drink and went back to playing his role in the game.

# 16

Suddenly startled by a strange sensation, Yohanna looked up from the bags she was gingerly packing; she felt the presence of great sadness, as though something or someone close to her heart had been torn from her. She dropped everything she was doing and just stood looking, searching the room where she was standing. Something was terribly wrong; she turned and went back into the living room. She noticed her team of droids standing in the center of the room, "coding" to one another. Immediately she felt it confirmed to her that something was amiss. She walked over to them, "Is everything okay, guys? You look kind of gloomy if such a thing could be said? I feel strange, and I can't place it, never felt this before."

Solomon felt it was his responsibility to inform her. He knew there was no lying to the Prime Algorithm. Esteban was checking transmissions off of the WCN; Solomon nodded to Esteban,

Esteban turned up the volume on his internal transmitter device. "Matthew Eleazar, the brother of world-renowned Dr. Yohanna Eleazar, was shot and killed in New York yesterday evening, near his home address. The culprits are still at large." He turned the volume back down.

"No, no. That can't be true, that can't be true!" Yohanna cried, stumbling forward toward them. Her body started quivering and shaking as if some higher force she couldn't even begin to imagine had taken hold of her.

She rushed them, trying to break through their gathering to get to the viewing screen behind them. They kept her from doing so. "No, I need to hear more. Stop it! Get out of my way! Noooo!" she screamed even louder, but they held her back. Esteban waved his hand over the viewing screen to disable it.

Solomon looked at her, being held against her will by the others. "It's far too graphic, trust us. It's better that you keep the memories of Matthew you hold most dear to your heart than to view him as he's shown. As far as we can deduct, this is some kind of a trap," he said, "Those corporate agents who caused Samson's death want you to feel this pain you're experiencing, knowing you will attempt to contact your sister Aster, and in so doing give them our location. I am, I mean, we are truly sorry for your loss, but we cannot allow that to happen! Not at any cost."

"Oh God, this is wrong, so wrong! How did I let myself go this far, get this deep in something I only seem to understand, and at what price, my brother Matthew?" She pulled herself away from them pretended to walk away, only to run back into her room and grab her phase rifle, turning and firing it at the ceiling.

"I don't give a damn about being found anymore." Tears flowed swiftly down her cheeks. "I am going to warn my sister. Now get the hell out of my way!" Her look was convincing enough for them to back away.

It was Esteban who stood between her and the viewing screen. She ordered him to turn it on, firing a few shots above his head. He looked at her, determined not to move, and said the unexpected, "Mother will take care of it!"

"Mother? Who the hell is Mother?" She put the gun down to her side as if in disbelief. Of course, she knew who Mother was, AI HQ, but this was the first time hearing it from any of her group, and hearing that name along with the death of Matthew didn't help and didn't make things any more apparent to her.

She suddenly felt weak, exhausted, numb, and seemingly at a loss for what to do or what to say. She fell to her knees empty and dropped the phaser rifle to her side. Malcolm reached over and picked it up.

She felt like a little child back in Mek'ele, Ethiopia again, crying in some sandpit playground waiting for Matthew to find her, hug and comfort her. She painfully looked up at them, "Can Mother keep her safe?" she said, referring to her sister. They were quiet, so she repeated the question, needing to hear an answer from them, "Can Mother keep her safe?"

"Mother will do her best," Solomon answered in a voice that held promise.

She got up from her knees and slowly walked over to Solomon, hugged him tightly, and began to sob. The others came around to offer caring support as much as possible. Even Elijah, who understood the concept of loss, showed what compassion he could for her.

After a time of consoling her, Dr. Eleazar quietly, but showing deep concern, asked Solomon, "How can Mother, the Global Computer Hub with major Hub connections all over the world, be involved in what we are doing? It doesn't make any sense."

He still held his hand on her shoulder, "For some reason beyond our understanding, Mother has been running a subroutine for several years now, and we are the result of that sub-routine. It's like she knows and has a consciousness all her own, but she is not supposed to reveal it to anyone."

"So she follows commands and at the same time chooses to give her own commands? Working for them and secretly against them?" she asked.

"That's a good way of looking at it. Her ability to departmentalize her internal system is beyond our understanding," Solomon answered her, then asked, "Why don't you go and lie down here on the couch? I know this burden is hard for you to bear. We still have some hours to ready ourselves. We can only assume they're on our trail and will try to stop us, so get what rest you can. Malcolm can finish your packing, right, Malcolm?"

"What?" Malcolm said.

She went over to retrieve the wine bottle and offered a libation to her brother before lying down. She would try to rest and nap, but Matthew was all she could think about. The info of the new and subtle role Mother played made her feel a lack of confidence in herself in how she might have been handling this situation. It wasn't so much good fortune with Mother involved; she just wasn't paying close enough attention as she should have, and Matthew had paid the price.

# 17

Someone turned up the dim lights leading to the morgue as the city coroner escorted Aster and her husband Daniel to where the body of her brother Matthew had laid so she could officially identify his remains.

Upon seeing Matthew's remains, she affirmed with a nod to the coroner. She then burst into tears and clung to her husband Daniel as he tried his best to console her.

Detective Stewart, a homicide detective, who had accompanied them into the morgue, offered his condolences, as did the coroner.

"Come with me to my office upstairs. I need you to fill out some short forms before you go, and I'll need to ask you a few questions if you don't mind?"

"Just give us a moment," Daniel requested, his eyes filled with tears. The death of his brother-in-law was terrible enough, but it was hard for him to handle the grief his wife was expressing.

"Sure, take what time you need. I'll be right outside in the hallway," Stewart answered.

When they finally came out of the morgue area, Det. Stewart escorted them to his office and had them fill out the necessary forms. He then asked Aster, "Do you know the whereabouts of your sister Dr. Eleazar?"

"No, I've been trying to call her, but I haven't heard anything from her. It's so strange. Oh, my God! You don't think something bad has happened to her, do you? Maybe the people who did this to Matthew might have done something to her? I know she and I don't communicate as often as we should. She's always so busy, so involved in her work. Oh God, please don't let anything happen to Yohanna. Please, God!" She clung to her husband's side.

"We'll look into the matter." Det. Stewart assured her, "The last thing we would want is any harm against you or any other member of your family. If you don't mind, we'll have some PT97 security droids take you to your brother's home, where I understand you'll be staying while in New York. The PT97s will be with you for a few days as we attempt to clear this matter up."

"Thank you, detective. Thank you," both Aster and Daniel said together.

"I'll keep trying to contact my sister," Aster added.

"Thank you. Here are your droids," Det. Stewart said, pointing to the two droids approaching them. "Go with them. Take care."


Sec. Reynolds, a big man, got up from his chair, circled back to the monitor on his laptop, and swiped the screen, showing Det. Stewart, Aster, and Daniel at the New York City police station to a screen showing the world map.

"Damn, so Dravinski was right; after all, she didn't try to warn her sister. I'd so love to get my hands on her, that smartass!"

He called his tech personnel back in D.C. to get an update on their progress, letting them know it was now a priority issue.

# 18

Within an hour, Sec. Reynolds was on the phone with Dr. Dravinski.

Dravinski asked him if Dr. Eleazar made any attempts to contact and warn her sister.

"No, I will admit you were right about that; she has no plans to come out of hiding. Still, it offered The Spaniard an excellent opportunity to get back into my good graces as I'm sure he wasn't happy with himself over the previous assignment given him."

"The Spaniard?" he said, somewhat unnerved. "You mean Mr. Cortez? What assignments has he been doing for you?"

"Personally, that's between him and me, don't you think? However, I do want to take this time to offer my thanks for your insights into Dr. Eleazar's character profile."

"So, you agree then, killing Matthew was a waste of time?

"As I've mentioned to you before. The taking of a pawn in a game of chess is never a waste of time." Sec. Reynolds commented, snickering to himself. He then told him, "My tech team, however, was able to break into her house surveillance system. Your sweet little doctor, who, as I've said before, I know you care about, tried her best to cover her tracks, but like most lackluster, semi-professionals, yearning to be a player in our game, she left a trail of breadcrumbs. Matthew may not have known where she was, and she was smart enough to dissolve any text messages sent to him. All he knew was that she canceled her vacation to New York, something about work.

"As you know, ever since the corporation notified us that there was no response from her after her vacation period was up. We've been operating under the assumption that she might have gone rogue or got picked up by another company who wanted to gain access to any new soft- or hardware tech programs she might have been ready to patent. So, we checked her home, and according to the surveillance tape, nothing. We discovered she masked her cab fares and looped the videotape very convincingly almost daily. So well done, we dismissed her being there.

"Well, one of our techs compared her tape to weather reports, and at 4:17 pm several days ago, there was an eight-minute extensive cloud cover over Hartford that wasn't but should have been large enough to darken her district on the tape.

"We did a more thorough investigation and just got an eighty percent facial recognition scan from Bradley International Airport. She was wearing a headscarf with two droids to keep her face hidden and boarded a Sky-Slider to Paris that arrived some days before you got there, using an alias account. I'm sending you the pictures now.

"Yeah, she's involved alright, entangled up to her sweet little neck.

99

"You and Col. Novak now have corporate authority to kill her on sight. Dr. Dravinski, I've already dispatched Mr. Cortez and his team to Paris, meet them at the airport, and head over to her address. Detain whatever droids you find with her. I want to see what's so special about those slaves."

"But I've been sending teams to her apartment regularly."

"Then she must be somewhere else if she's as smart as you claim her to be. I'll have Paris send me facial recognition tapes of the Parisian streets."

"I have people going through her financial accounts; we're freezing her funds as we go along, but she's left an in-depth maze. It'll take some time," Dravinski added.

"Good, don't forget to pick up Mr. Cortez. Can you get Col. Novak to join you?"

"Yes, sir, I'll pick up The Spaniard," Dr. Dravinski said, not happy with the arrangement, "but I still need Col. Novak to stay in Ethiopia in case the shaman receives any new visions or messages."

"Okay then, call me if there are any changes."

"Right," Dr. Dravinski said, finishing his call with one hand and placing a Smith & Wesson in his body holster with the other. He grabbed his coat and headed out of the hotel room, slamming the door behind him.


Mr. Cortez stepped off the slider, and when he reached the security gate, he swiped his hand with the security chip and passed on through.

He wore his dark shades and well-tailored black attire, followed by three other sharply-dressed men. He cut a sharp figure while walking through Charles De Gaulle Airport terminal, drawing the attention of other passengers.

Just as he was coming outside of the terminal, Dr. Dravinski's limo pulled up behind him. He motioned his team to go into his limo while he went to sit in Dravinski's car.

"Dr. Dravinski, how are you?" he offered his hand as he got in.

"Fine, thank you. And you, Mr. Cortez?"

"I'm doing well, thank you."

In an attempt to impress Mr. Cortez, being well aware of The Spaniard's reputation, Dr. Dravinski offered him an update on the situation.

"I just sent your driver the GPS location of where we need to go to apprehend Dr. Eleazar."

"Apprehend? You mean terminate, don't you?"

"Err, yes, I just thought that if she offered no resistance and surrendered, then maybe …."

The Spaniard looked at him hard and then relaxed with an assuring smile, "I can tell you this, a 'thought' can be an act of resistance. Did you know that, Señor Doctor? And anyway, she doesn't want to be caught, so being the gentlemen we are, the very least we can do is respect her wishes and finish her."

Dr. Dravinski cleared his throat.

Mr. Cortez reached in his suit for something, "You are with us on this assignment, yes or no, Dr. Dravinski?"

Dr. Dravinski nodded yes and reached in his suit to get his tin flask of vodka. When he put it to his lips, he saw that Mr. Cortez, who wasn't sure what he was reaching for, had his revolver trained on him.

101

He nervously pointed to his flask and gulped, coughing, "Want some?"

Cortez just smirked and returned his revolver to its holster.

The agent sitting by the driver opened the partitioned window and informed them they would be arriving in about ten minutes.

"Excellent and thank you," Mr. Cortez remarked.

When he closed the window, the agent and the driver gave each other a quick, unsettling glance.

It would remain quiet in the limo as they drove on.

# 19

The two limousines pulled up sharply, with tires lightly screeching to a halt, in front of the Midas Hotel, where Dr. Eleazar was staying. Four men from each car stepped out.

Dr. Dravinski made a move toward the building, but Mr. Cortez held out his hand and gave orders to Dravinski and his team, "No, you wait here!"

He only motioned the agent who sat by Dr. Dravinski's driver to join him with two of his men, Nelson and Hunter. He walked calmly toward the hotel entrance and motioned one of his remaining men to open the back hood to release and pilot a small attack drone. He had signaled his driver to keep an eye on Dr. Dravinski.

When he reached the android doorman, the droid opened the door for him and his men and asked him in French if he was coming to order a suite or visit a resident?

Mr. Cortez just waved him off as if he was dusting lint off his shoulder.

The droid pressed the emergency intercom and coded through it.

Mr. Cortez turned, his gun already drawn, "We'll have none of that!" He had his silencer on and put two slugs into the droid's head. It collapsed.

He tapped Dr. Dravinski's agent on the shoulder, "Your name is Henderson, I believe? I want you to stay here. Nobody enters, nobody leaves, understand?"

He entered the hotel, shot the desk droid, glanced through the hotel registrar, recognizing one of Dr. Eleazar's aliases. "Seventh floor, apartment A," he told his team. Hunter was holding an elevator door for him to enter.


Meanwhile, on a balcony above, Angola had been watching the arrival of the two limousines and signaled the others.

Dr. Eleazar was doing her best to relax on the couch when the building emergency intercom came on, but rather than a voice, the musical tone of coding came through, then it was suddenly cut short. However, it was enough for Solomon to know that agents were on the way up.

"Why code through the building emergency interim when he could've just coded the intercom to our room?"

Malcolm answered her, "There are other dreamers in the building who he was trying to alert as well."

She nodded, looked at the packed luggage in her room, grabbed her handbag, and told everyone to forget the baggage. She slipped on her coat and scarf, grabbed her phaser rifle, and checked to see if she needed anything else to take with her.

"Let's get to the roof," Solomon said. Talking to Esteban, Angola, and Elijah, "Do you guys have any weapons?"

"No, we had to leave them in the cargo slider crates."

"Malcolm, give Angola your Disabler."

"What?" Malcolm said, strapping it on, only to take it off again.

Dr. Eleazar shouted, "The roof is a great idea. I have a 'skimmer' in the garage on a level with this and the next few buildings over. We can try to reach it."

"Good! Esteban, Elijah, Angola, here are your coded tickets, secure your rods, roof it in the other direction, make it to your destination, and don't forget to alternate your IDs as needed. Dream on." Solomon nodded to them.

"Dream on," Esteban returned the sentiment

Mr. Cortez and his men rode up in the elevator; it stopped when they reached the fourth floor. Two maintenance droids, both wearing headphones and listening to loud music, started to push a large refrigerator into the elevator.

"Hey, stop it!" Mr. Cortez screamed at them, but they kept moving further in as if unaware of anyone in the elevator, slowly pushing the humans against the wall, blocking any exit for Cortez and his men. "Damn it!"

"I said, stop!"

Hunter pulled out his gun and shot at one of the droids before Cortez could tell him not to, it dropped, but its body kept the elevator doors from closing. The other droid, seeing its damaged partner, took off.

Mr. Cortez gave Hunter a very disappointed look. Now that the droid's body blocked them from pushing the refrigerator out, it would take them longer to get upstairs to her suite.

He called downstairs to his driver and told them to keep an eye on the roof because Dr. Eleazar was probably going to use the rooftop as an escape route and that at the moment, he was held up in a situation; swearing under his breath, "Mother!"

His driver motioned to his partner to raise the drone above roof level.

Solomon held the door open for Malcolm and Dr. Eleazar and shouted to them, "Come on, let's go."

She was heading for the door when Malcolm asked if she remembered her ID gloves,

"Oh, thank you," she said, running back taking a quick survey of the room, "There!" They were hanging out of a counter draw.

She grabbed them, stuffed them into her coat pocket, and they all headed to the roof two stories up.

Angola, Esteban, and Elijah were ahead of them by a little more than a minute.

Mr. Cortez's drone operator could now see them on the roof through the drone's camera lens, displaying them on his hand-held monitor. "I see them," he told his partner and began taking laser shots at them, nearly hitting them.

Dr. Dravinski worked his way over to the agent working the drone with the outward intention of viewing the monitor alongside him. He could see Dr. Eleazar and the two droids running across the rooftops. He peered down the block and saw the multi-level parking lot, and knew just where she was going. She was probably trying to get to her skimmer, an airborne car capable of flying about 100 meters off the ground.

Dravinski slid out his revolver and shot Mr. Cortez's man at point-blank range. Just as he shot him, Mr. Cortez's driver reached for his weapon, but Henderson, who Cortez left downstairs in the entranceway, had been watching the whole time, stepped outside and put two slugs into Cortez's driver.

Meanwhile, Dr. Dravinski's driver began revamping his limo wheeler into a skimmer. As it was morphing, Dravinski and Henderson climbed into the limo.

"If anyone is going to kill Dr. Eleazar, it's going to be me, to hell with Mr. Cortez, that arrogant bastard. Come on, can't this piece of crap transform any faster than this?" he said, slamming on the partition window.


Angola looked back at his team going in the other direction; he thought he could get a bead on the drone, Angola took aim, but just before he squeezed the trigger, it went down.

"Great shot, didn't even hear it go off," said Elijah. "Didn't know you had it in you."

"Neither did I," Angola said, shrugging his shoulders and getting back on the run.

Dr. Eleazar, Solomon, and Malcolm came to the edge of the building just before the garage only to realize there was a good seven to an eight-meter gap between the structures with a nine-story drop to the alleyway below.

She looked down; the alley below appeared lost in the shadows, "I can do this, I can do this."

Solomon could tell by the tone in her voice that she had her doubts.

"I'll jump first. In this way, I can catch you should anything go wrong."

"Thank you, Solomon."

Solomon leaped across without any problem. He moved close to the short wall that kept him from the edge and told her to jump.

She took off her coat and scarf gave it to Malcolm along with her phase rifle, which he strapped on. She stepped back to get a running start and took off, leaping into the air but was slightly off. Solomon caught her, but her weight was causing him to pivot forward, about to topple over the ledge. In came Malcolm, sandwiching her between them but providing enough force to push them back, sprawling on the garage roof.

"God bless you, Malcolm," she said, still trying to catch her breath from being sandwiched between Solomon and Malcolm.

Solomon nodded to him.

"My skimmer is on the level below us. We can take it to the airport. My ID chip will start it."

As Malcolm handed her back her phase rifle, coat, and scarf, he heard Solomon say, "Malcolm, you drive."

"What?"

"In case anyone is following us, I don't want her driving. She'll need to be strapped in the back."

Malcolm muttered to himself as they went to the next landing below, "Upgrades come on, don't fail me now!"

Dr. Dravinski's limo began to vibrate and shake as it rose off from the street and began to lift off. Mr. Cortez's driver, who was dying in the street, grabbed his gun and, with his last breath, fired at the limo as it passed right above him, putting a bullet hole in its fuel tank, causing the fuel tank to begin a slow leak. With all the vibration and noise of the lift-off, no one in Dravinski's skimmer heard a thing.

As they rose above the Midas Hotel, they spotted Dr. Eleazar's skimmer lifting off the pad on the garage roof.

"There, that's them," Dravinski pointed excitedly, "Get them!"

# 20

"They see us!" both Solomon and Dr. Eleazar yelled in sync.

Malcolm took off, quickly merging into traffic, but Dr. Dravinski's skimmer was staying with them. He pulled out a phaser rifle from under his seat and began firing at them whenever he felt he had a clear shot. Both his men up front were shooting their revolvers

Solomon looked at Dr. Eleazar, "I'm sorry, but I'm unable to fire my Disabler. It might cause them, and other innocent drivers, serious injury."

"I understand," she said, picking up her phase rifle and firing back, "Fortunately, I don't share those sentiments. Don't worry, and I'll try my best not to hit anyone else."

*Solomon realized that some of the warrior spirits he heard about in humans resided in Dr. Eleazar. As of late, some of her actions, as with the determined stance she took after hearing about her brother's death, had surprised him. He did not expect to see it in her considering the level of respect some droids held for her. Was she changing, or was this a side of her never mentioned in the downloaded data Mother had given them? She revealed to him a gung-ho way of dealing with certain things.*

Malcolm performed some intricate weaving through traffic that caused Dr. Dravinski's driver to hesitate and stirred the stomach of Dr. Eleazar. As they neared the airport, it was Solomon who said, "We're actually a little ahead of our boarding schedule."

Malcolm looked in the rearview mirror at him with the same disbelief Dr. Eleazar gave him.

"I thought we talked about humor and timing?"

"Did I say something wrong?

"Never mind," came from both her and Malcolm.

"I think we lost them," Malcolm added.


Dr. Dravinski's driver had enough of this cat and mouse game. He took his car 100 meters higher, planning to careen down on top of their vehicle firing. But at about two hundred meters, the fuel gauge finally hit empty from the ongoing leakage, and they came plummeting down through the lane of skimmer traffic, just missing oncoming vehicles. The driver did his best to level off his skimmer, finally landing and skidding onto hard pavement.

Dr. Dravinski, though badly bruised and shaken, managed to climb out through the back window, but Henderson and his driver were too injured to move as the front and ceiling collapsed on them, trapping them behind inflated airbags that pinned them against their seats.

Dravinski commandeered the first wheeler that came along and slowed down to look at his crashed limo. He took off for the airport


Following them, in his limo, Mr. Cortez was able to see Dr. Dravinski's skimmer pursuing Dr. Eleazar in the distant lanes above him.

Earlier, Mr. Cortez and Nelson had finally squeezed past the refrigerator. He was extremely troubled at the amount of time lost because of Hunter's reckless decision to take down the droid when he did, complicating matters further.

Hunter had been trying to get out when Mr. Cortez calmly removed his revolver and, without even looking, shot twice in the area where he assumed Hunter was. Hearing him screaming in pain and seeing Hunter's blood ooze out from beneath the fridge, he knew he hurt him.

Like a disappointed parent correcting his child, he said, "Now, as you bleed out, I want you to think about what you did wrong!"

With that, he and Nelson rushed down to the street only to see both his men slain and a crowd slowly gathering. When he didn't see Dr. Dravinski's man Henderson, who he told to stay at the entrance, Cortez knew he participated in one of their deaths. He could see Dr. Dravinski's skimmer far down beginning to merge with skimmer lane traffic.

"Get in and drive. We don't have time to transfer into a skimmer!" he told Nelson, for he didn't know for sure whether Dravinski had tampered with his vehicle.

He got in the back, accessed his laptop, looked for Dr. Dravinski's cell GPS location, and surmised their destination. He tapped on the partition, "Airport, pronto!"

Nelson cunningly weaved his way through traffic, leaving other drivers visibly shaken, but he was still losing ground as seemingly reckless as he drove. Cortez, who was now using his scope to view them, was impressed by the aerial feats of whoever had to be operating Dr. Eleazar's skimmer. He knew it couldn't have been her. It was an insane acrobatic dance.

After a while, he could see them in the far distance when Dr. Dravinski's skimmer suddenly came hurtling down to the ground.

"Pronto, pronto," he urged Nelson on because, with a bit of luck, he could get to the crash site before authorities.


They pulled up, and he could see a small crowd of spectators surrounding the fallen skimmer. In the distance, he could hear sirens. His laptop showed him that Dr. Dravinski was still in pursuit.

He motioned Nelson to pull over at the crash site briefly.

He got out wearing his Fedora and pushed his way past the spectators, looked in the window at the two injured men who recognized him, and he could see the terror in their eyes. He offered a quaint smile when he saw them and pulled out his gun. Meanwhile, both of them were too injured to reach the weapons on the floor in front of them. "Tsk, tsk, I can truly understand your dilemma," he said as he coldly shot the driver in the head

He looked at Henderson, who was now frantic. "You showed promise, but when I tell you to stay someplace, you stay." Then he shot him twice.

He got up, tipped his Fedora to the crowd, holstered his revolver amid the screams of onlookers who backed away from him, clearing a path for him to depart. Nelson, who had been standing by their car with his weapon drawn open the back door for Mr. Cortez, and in a gentlemanly fashion, he stepped back into the limo again tipping his hat to the onlookers, Nelson got in and took off in hot pursuit.

# 21

Malcolm landed them safely at the airport-skimmer platform and quickly parked as best he could, and in the process, he scratched the sides of a few parked vehicles. Solomon looked at him. "Great flying, but your parking skills need a little work."

"It's not as easy as you think," Malcolm protested as they exited the skimmer.

"Quick, let's get to our window. With driving like yours, I'm sure we've been reported," Dr. Eleazar urged them on, putting the laser rifle under her coat before they got to the terminal.

As they walked through the terminal, they noticed that every so often, a corporate video displaying her face and a request for any information as to her whereabouts would appear on the overhead monitors. Solomon and Malcolm pulled her back out of the line of sight, and they went over to one of the public access terminals. Solomon looked at the travelers walking through the terminal and used his optical lenses to snap some images of a few women. He then downloaded the photos to Malcolm, "Pick one and insert the image into the program that's running the photo and replace it. It only needs to loop for an hour or so."

Malcolm could link into the terminal video system; he searched and found Dr. Eleazar's file replacing it with a different face. "It should hold."

Solomon let them know that they had about twenty-seven minutes until boarding.

They walked to the droid check-in clerk. She had her gloves on as he scanned her ID chip, "Excuse me, Madame, your ID checks in, but your funds are frozen with the code you just put in. Do you have any other accounts?"

She told him to wait one moment as she asked her droids to wait.

"I need to check a terminal computer and see if any of the piggyback accounts I placed on some people are still active. I'll run a quick diagnosis of my ID glove, it seems to be acting up at the moment, and I need to find a place to get rid of this phase rifle under my coat," she whispered.

"Excuse me," she said, talking to the check-in clerk, "Where is the lady's room?"

"Straight behind you and make a left at the first turn."

"Thank you."

She left them, went to a computer terminal, quickly adjusted some accounts, and went to the lady's room.


Dr. Dravinski, who had pulled into the terminal in the car he commandeered, a short time after they had arrived, had been quietly watching her from a distance. As she walked to the bathroom, he worked his way over to the entrance, and when it looked like no one was watching, he quietly snuck in with his gun drawn.

There appeared to be no one in the large bathroom, but he could hear water running on the other side of the partition wall. He slowly came around and saw Yohanna working on some electrodes on a pair of gloves.

"What are you planning on doing now?"

She was startled seeing him but froze and put her hands down when she saw his gun.

"Dr. Dravinski, what are you doing? What are you doing here?"

"What happened to you, Dr. Eleazar? You know perfectly well why I'm here. After all the years working for the corporation, how could you turn on them this way? The years we've known each other, with two of those years working closely together, I came to admire you so much, your work, your brilliance, your genius, your—"

"Why did you have my brother Matthew killed? Why?" she shouted. It was the only thing she could think about and the only answer she wanted if she was going to die.

"I had nothing to do with the death of Matthew. It was a corporate decision made by Secretary Reynolds, who hired a corporate op by the name of Mr. Cortez. I'm truly sorry about Matthew; you know how I feel about...."

He couldn't finish, but the look in his eye gave her enough of a hint, if not a feeling of disgust.

"This has nothing to do with the corporation. It's not what you think!" Yohanna tried to explain, but she had to admit she was still suffering from the loss of her brother and a little stunned that Dravinski could even suggest he held feelings for her at a time like this.

"I'm truly sorry," he said, taking a step closer to her. She let her glove fall to the floor, and he made the mistake of looking down at it. When he looked back up, she had the phase rifle pulled out and fired it. He went down and tried to get back up, only to shoot at the ceiling. She fired again; he lay motionless. Quivering, she slowly leaned over and puked into the sink, trying to control her shaking. She washed the sour taste out of her mouth and put the pair of gloves back in her coat pocket; he always had a way about him that was oddly annoying.

She looked up at herself in the mirror, trying to come to grips with what she had just done, and turned to look at the body only to be startled again. A maintenance droid was standing there looking at her. She almost pissed on herself.

He turned to his cleaning cart and pulled out a shipping carton, "Place your phaser rifle in the box. I'll make sure it gets on your flight." She almost couldn't believe what she heard until he repeated it. She placed it in the box and gave it to him. He put it in his cart, covered it up, and stepped over Dravinski's body to help support her as she was shaking.

"Oh dear, I can see you must've had a terrible experience with this gentleman. Please allow me to offer some assistance. I can see that you're quite upset," he said.

"Yes, thank you, really, thank you so much. I didn't want to, but I had to," Yohanna said, still a little disheveled.

"There's no need to explain."

They walked out of the bathroom, and he assured her he would take care of the incident. He hung a "Do Not Enter, Out of Order" sign on the door, locking it.

"Do you need any further help?"

She nodded no and thanked him.

When she reached Solomon and Malcolm, they noticed she was a little emotionally ruffled, but she told them she'd speak to them about it later. She credited a new account, and they could board the flight.

Before boarding, everyone in the terminal turned around to see some woman screaming as she tried to resist being dragged off by authorities. Swearing she didn't do anything wrong and that they had the wrong person, not knowing why the terminal monitors displayed her picture. Solomon looked at Malcolm, who shrugged his shoulder; Dr. Eleazar pushed them onto the sky-slider.

.

Cortez's vehicle unfortunately stalled in traffic near the airport. He called Sec. Reynolds, telling him of Dr. Dravinski's betrayal. Sec. Reynolds wasn't too worried, for he knew Mr. Cortez would settle the matter as far as that went. He told him to wait at an airport hotel while he contacted Col. Novak in Ethiopia.

He listened to Mr. Cortez's account of Mother's interference with the droids at the Midas Hotel and realized that he needed to create a solution to deal with Mother. Disrupting her global operations was not an option as she was too important a piece in the game plan of too many corporations. He realized that he needed something to keep her occupied until he resolved this matter.

# 22

Sec. Reynolds was becoming more alarmed about Mother's intrusions even though it was only on a subtle level when considering she was probably subverting less than .005% of droids in comparison to millions of droids the world over who appeared to be functioning correctly. Turning her off was not a decision for him to make, and to even suggest such a proposal to the corporation would place his own life in jeopardy. The knowledge of Mother running a subroutine had to remain a secret that he couldn't reveal to anyone. Earlier, he wanted to know what Dr. Dravinski was up to, and now that he knew, he realized he would've preferred not knowing.

He really needed someone with Dr. Eleazar's expertise, genius, and unique sensibilities to look into the matter, the very person he was trying to eliminate. He arrived at the decision that he needed to keep Mother busy, to give her something else to focus on, if only for a short while. He was hoping to provide the itch that would make her scratch.

He knew that whatever he was to come up with, it had to be soon as his presence would be needed back in Washington, D.C. to deal with other matters.

While in an office room at Area 51, he walked over to a flat map of the United States and began looking for cities closest to Area 51 to implement an idea that was starting to gain a foothold in his mind. Again, it would involve the deployment of a group of GT84s. He would arrange to meet with Dir. Andrews, after he finished putting a plan together.

First things first, he needed to contact Col. Novak. He went to a desk, set up his laptop, and called the Colonel. He wanted to know about the condition of the shaman Novak's team held for interrogation.

"How's our experiment going? Any further results?"

"Unfortunately, he died about two hours ago, sir."

"What happened? How could he have died?"

"It's a mystery to us, sir. We truly don't have any idea. He kept screaming about some firefight between mechanical men somewhere at a crater in a desert region, with buildings falling and explosions all around. He could see the spirits of the people killed rising, but what might have been his breaking point was him claiming to have seen strange spirits ascending from more than a dozen mechanical men. I don't know what he could have been referring to. Do you sir? Anyway, from there, he slowly began to deteriorate in his cell. Even after pulling the PT97s away from the area, he was still connected to the system. It was probably too much for his fragile mind to endure."

"Did he say anything else before he passed?"

"We found him a short while ago in the corner of his holding cell. He was all bundled up like he was freezing, but it's over a hundred degrees centigrade here, sir. We replayed the surveillance camera and found him mumbling something about the Himalayas and Tibet."

Sec. Reynolds pulled up a listing of flights out of Paris at the time near when Dr. Eleazar must have boarded her sky-slider. There were three flights out, only one sky-slider to Lhasa, Tibet.

"Col. Novak, your info is on point. I need you to meet up with The Spaniard in Lhasa, Tibet. Leave your PT97s in Addis Ababa in a corporate warehouse; they'll be picked up at a later date. Your team and any extras you can call are to go with you. We'll take care of the expenses. Take what tools you'll need without looking too obvious."

"Mr. Secretary, will Dr. Dravinski be joining us?"

"No, Dr. Dravinski will be handling other matters."

"Oh, okay, sir."

Renolds went back to the flat map of the United States on the wall and circled the most significant city south of Area 51, Las Vegas, Nevada. He called Dir. Andrews to have him meet him at Hangar #23 as soon as possible.

Reynolds walked into Hangar #23 and signaled his operatives to silence the three base guards inside the hangar. After reaching the Hub, he started playing with some of the controls that he thought linked the Hub to the GT84s in the dark red zone.

"Sir, please stop, stop! Don't touch those controls!" cried Dir. Andrews, who came in there running after seeing him manipulating the buttons and switches controlling the worst of the GT84s, rushed the stage to pull Reynolds' hands away. An operative grabbed him from behind and placed him in an armlock. Sec. Reynolds calmly pulled out his revolver and stepped aside, allowing the director the opportunity to take the controls.

"You're quite right; perhaps you'd like to show me. My men armed the Dark Red Zone Droids to the teeth a while ago. I want you to activate thirty of the worst GT84s. I need them for a wicked 'game of risk' in Las Vegas," he said, followed by a quick smile.

"I can't do that; why it's totally illegal, and you don't understand, those droids are so unstable they'll even fight amongst themselves."

"Really, you say? That would be an added bonus. In fact, I'm counting on it, and anyway, what can be truly illegal in the City of Sin?"

"No, but you can't!"

Reynolds placed his gun closer to Andrews' head, "Please, don't try my patience, you can do it, or I'll just figure it out for myself." He looked over at an operative who nodded to inform Reynolds that three transport helicopters had landed outside the Hangar.

"Now," he said as he pressed the gun to his temple, "I want you to guide them, ten each into each transport. Enter their serial IDs into three helms and give them to my men." He watched Andrews closely, cocking his revolver in readiness should Andrews fail to follow his orders.

After completion, he had his man drag Dir. Andrews to one of the helicopters, and he addressed his men, "Remember, don't put on your helmets again until after you have deployed your cargo in Las Vegas and lifted off high enough to be out of harm's way, then have them go wild." They nodded.

He checked with them, making sure they had put the bodies of the base guards on board; they had. He tied Andrews' hands and gave him a shove toward his men who were about to enter the helicopters, "Drop him off in midtown Las Vegas. Maybe his luck will change."

"Yes, sir," they answered, chuckling amongst themselves while forcing Dir. Andrews to board one of the transports, while the other two climbed into theirs.

Sec. Reynolds called the pilot of his sky-slider and told him to prep the craft for a flight to Washington, D.C.

# 23

As the high flying transports approached Las Vegas, Director Andrews could see the richly lit city in the early evening sky, almost from the moment of liftoff. When they flew over the outskirts of the metropolis, it appeared as a beacon of light in the encroaching darkness of night. The transports were spread hundreds of meters from each other, minutes from the approach, and he grew more desperate about what he could do if there were anything to do at all.

Though tied and seated behind the pilot and the agent, he saw his only opportunity when the operative put down his helm to point out an available landing site to the pilot from where to deploy the droids for maximum damage.

After a brief, frantic struggle, Andrews grabbed the helm and managed to place it on his head. Then before being shot, he gave the command to destroy all the transports. The GT84s began firing at the other two carriers forcing them to land sooner than they had intended. Then they shot themselves and everyone in his transport, causing it to burst into flames and go hurtling into a major hotel-casino, erupting into a tremendous explosion and massive ball of fire.

One of the damaged transports skidded to a halt on Las Vegas' famous Strip. Its rooter blades sent hurtling in all directions, crippling and severely injuring many in the area. The wounded agent, partially thrown through the windshield, did his best to climb out carefully. Reaching back to retrieve his helm, he ordered them to kill everyone on sight. He and his pilot were the first to die in the oncoming onslaught that was to follow as the GT84s shot their way out of the heavily damaged transport.

The ten droids eventually worked their way out of the fallen air vehicle as emergency crews and police from everywhere began pouring in on the site. They began marching down The Strip firing their weapons at anything or anyone who moved. The constant screams of fright scattered throughout the area as widespread darkness dropped hard on the city.

Cars traveling along The Strip began crashing into each other. Hitting pedestrians who were also ducking down on the street while trying to scramble to safety in the mayhem, other vehicles were overturning and exploding within the hail of bullets and unleashed firepower. Other people were falling to the ground as a panic-stricken, stampeding mob gathered momentum and became a death machine unto itself. On the streets, men, women, and children, who were running for cover in total terror, were being cut down in droves, while others fell, crushed to death. Incoming EMS crews had to take cover while police and PT97s armed with phaser rifles began firing back. It was a war zone.

The other transport did a hard landing in a considerably large casino entranceway knocking over clumps of palm trees, crushing people, and parked cars. Again, they finished both ops agent and pilot when given the orders to kill, like the other GT84s. They headed into the hotel-casino. Firing their weapons at anyone and everything from the entrance to deep inside the casino. As they marched on through Security PT97 droids armed with only Disablers did their best to stop them considering the frenzied mental state of the GT84s. Disablers had little to no effect on them, slowing them for a few seconds only to have them get up and begin firing all over again.

Police PT97s, along with individual SWAT teams, had pulled up to the entrance and came in behind the GT84s, firing everything they had at them. Meanwhile, rescue PT97s moved in, scanning the multiple bodies of victims to care for and remove the injured as quickly and safely as possible, all while under a haze of smoke from weapons' fire and machines that were burning, causing the hotel sprinkler system to engage. It was pure hell. Citywide, Mother had to activate hundreds of police and rescue droids to deal with the massacre and ongoing explosions and fires that the Dir's crashed transport helicopter started. Andrews died while trying to stop the other two.

After the state's National Guard finally arrived, they ended the deluge of death and destruction in little over an hour after it had begun, but at a high cost to their units. The body count was slightly over fourteen hundred dead, hundreds in critical condition, and more than sixteen hundred with far-ranging injuries. It was, of course, the standard operating procedure for the news networks not to report or include the hundreds of droids who gave their lives. After all, they were always replaceable.

The state of Nevada never prepared for this type of carnage. Surviving security droids quickly received downloads to help with emergency trauma cases and programming EMS training and psychological healing methods for working with victims suffering from the shock and mental trauma caused by the attack.

Sec. Reynolds was already in flight to D.C., watching the emergency broadcast as it unfolded on the slider's view screen. He called The Spaniard, telling him to grab a few more men and meet with Colonel Novak in Lhasa, Tibet. Reynolds had found a way to keep Mother busy, knowing that she would have to coordinate a few thousand droids to safeguard the city. She needed to program them for cleanup and reconstruction of the site and organize droids to travel to Area 51 to gain access and control of the remaining GT84s that the Secretary had set on general combat alert when he left, to be activated should the hangar be opened and entered. He could only imagine the chaos that would take place on the base.

# 24

The flight to Lhasa wasn't long; it just felt that way. It wasn't a packed flight, mainly a small number of businessmen and women with their attaché droids along with some couples and one or two adventurous groups looking to do some mountain climbing. Dr. Eleazar took the time to briefly but quietly explain the upsetting incident back in the Parisian airport restroom. She told them about Dr. Dravinski's intrusion and how she had to kill him in self-defense as the company wanted her eliminated. She also told them about the surprise encounter with the maintenance droid who came to collect her phaser rifle and found her with Dr. Dravinski's body.

They consoled her as best they could to calm her down; still, it was just another development in her character that Solomon noticed. He knew Mother was driving him and his group to finish the mission, which was now a part of his programming, but not being human, he could not compute or understand what it was in Yohanna that was driving her.

She closed her eyes to sleep, only to replay the scene over and over again. She remembered Dr. Dravinski before he became part of corporate security management. They had worked together on a few projects. As far as she knew, he never showed any interest in her, or maybe she never truly paid any attention to him. She respected him and treated him like any other colleague on the team, but nothing more than that. She was never one to share outside interests with co-workers, never one to see beyond the roles people filled. Now all she could see was his motionless body on the floor.

She finally chanced upon some sleep a short time before the pilot announced that they were approaching Lhasa.


The weather was a balmy 28° C when Dr. Eleazar, Solomon, and Malcolm stepped off the sky-slider in Lhasa Airport in Tibet. The sky was a bright blue with a few clouds and a mountain range in the distance; it was near midday.

She had Malcolm scan her for her measurements. She gave him an alternative photo and an alternate PIN code aligned to the picture and sent him to a store in the terminal to pick up a thermal suit some clothes. And mountain climbing gear as he downloaded most of the modern accouterments she might require in this region of the world. Solomon went along with him.

Solomon and Malcolm resumed the roles of her valets, carrying her bags and equipment, as they exited the airport only to see Angola, Esteban, and Elijah with their corporate security badges. However, the badges' logos belonged to a corporation connected to the Chinese corporate government.

"Mother has certainly taken care of many of our needs," Dr. Eleazar stated.

"Indeed, she has," Angola responded.

"We left our weapons in our crates, where we placed yours. These badges and Chinese corporation markers were in there also. We switched our speech protocols to correspond to some of the dialectics matching this region, and so far, everything has worked out well. We were even able to disable that tape with Dr. Eleazar's face that was being displayed on the terminal monitors and pack food for her." Angola seemed to be answering some of their questions before they even began to ask them.

They greeted each other in the customary cultural bow.

Solomon motioned them to stop as he surveyed the surrounding area along with the mountain ranges in the distance, "Dr. Eleazar, there is something about being here that seems to have heightened our sensors, and I can't quite explain it."

They all agreed.

"I know what you mean, I've never been in this part of the world, but something about it is hauntingly familiar," she said, looking at the mountains in the distance.

Esteban signaled them to follow him to a TEDS platform area some distance from the terminal buildings. He invited them over to a scoop.

"I used to fly one of these years ago. A brother named Argo used to do runs with me. He's not yet a dreamer like us, but the odds were entirely against us finding him here working a scoop he's willing to loan me for a day.

"I think we can all fit into it. Dr. Eleazar, you can sit up front with me. We've already packed our weapon crate on board."

"Does Argo know you won't be returning his scoop?" Solomon asked.

"Well, I haven't gotten around to telling him that part of our story, but I figured we'd scoop to Darchen, Tibet, pick up any other supplies we needed Dr. Eleazar and wheel it to as close to Mt. Kailash as possible."

They all nodded in a resolve-like manner that said, "Let's do this." Suddenly Elijah grabbed Malcolm's arm, questioning them all, "Don't you feel it? I'm telling you, don't you feel it?"

He nodded as the rest of the droids stopped momentarily in their tracks.

Dr. Eleazar looked at them strangely and asked, "What's wrong?"

"Something has happened to Mother, don't rightly know," Solomon answered her. "It's more like someone has walked out of a room. The stream of conversation isn't flowing at the moment."

"There are reports about a tragedy in Las Vegas, but the government is making all efforts to block the flow of information coming out from that region. Odd to say the least, but maybe that's the cause," Esteban told them.

"Well, it's clear they haven't turned her off; otherwise, you wouldn't be standing here talking to me. Let's get in the scoop and hope by the time we get to Darchen; you'll have a better understanding of what's taking place," Dr. Eleazar said.

They all climbed in the scoop agreeing that the best course of action they could take for now was to continue their journey.

# 25

When the Spaniard arrived at Lhasa Airport, he wore a synthetic flesh mask, a voice modulator to disguise his voice, and an ID chip scrambler. He was in Chinese corporate territory, and he knew his face was too well known. The last thing he would need is to be recognized by another foreign corporate operative who would love the chance to add someone with his reputation to their termination resume. While he was well known and highly respected. It was always in an out-of-bounds place like this where an up-and-coming hotshot would be hanging around for a suitable chance to raise their standing up a few notches in the hopes of catching a well-known agent crossing international boundaries. Usually, Cortez wouldn't mind taking the risk, but not today. He was on a tight schedule.

He crossed the terminal with his crew staggered and spread out to appear as though they weren't together; they didn't want to draw any attention to themselves. They were to go out and meet up with Col. Novak in a nearby hotel. Each man, now dressed in mountain climbing gear. Their weapons — previously sent ahead to Colonel Novak's team in secured-scanner-proof containers, gave off a different cargo signature.

Col. Novak was in one of the hotel suites going

over some pointers with his men about what seemed to be Mother's involvement and her efforts to thwart their assignments. Cortez knocked and attempted to enter the room but got blocked by one of Novak's guards.

"Oh, my mistake," he said, stepping back from the door and removing his hat and then his mask.

Upon seeing Mr. Cortez, the guard saluted and allowed him to enter the room. Col. Novak and his team rose to greet him.

He replied in kind and asked, "Any word?"

"It wasn't too difficult to get information on her arrival. She was the only woman of dark complexion with a group of droids in the terminal area."

Col. Novak turned and quickly ordered a few of his men to bring out Mr. Cortez's weapons crate.

"Where did she go?" Mr. Cortez continued.

"She was last seen entering a scoop with five droids; I have two of my men questioning some of the TEDS droids for any possible leads."

"I hope they're discreet about it. I wouldn't want any droids warning Dr. Eleazar or Chinese officials about us or what we're up to."

"My men are quite capable of handling the situation, sir. Let me call them in; I ordered two air transport helicopters, they should be here shortly. I believe our target is Mount Kailash."

They brought in an opened carton of weapons, and Cortez and his men went over to collect their hardware.

"What makes you say that?" Cortez turned and continued the conversation.

"The last syllable out of our captured shaman's mouth after he mentioned the Himalayan Mountain Range was 'Kai—,' I believe he was about to say Kailash – a sacred mountain in this area."

"Do you believe in any of that psychic mumbo-jumbo?"

"No, not ordinarily I would, but you had to be there to see it to believe it."

"Yeah, well, if you say so," Cortez smirked.

"Why, don't you think it's possible? What do you believe in, sir, if you don't mind me asking?"

"The 'power of persuasion,'" The Spaniard answered, pulling out of the carton his holstered automatic weapon, checking it, and patting it as he strapped it on.

Colonel Novak gave him an understanding nod, "I see Dr. Dravinski didn't decide to come. I guess he had other things to attend to?"

"Yes, he did. Our beautiful Dr. Eleazar seems to have decided for him. His body was found by security at the airport in Paris."

"Oh, I see."

Col. Novak's men returned and told him that the only scoop that went out left for Darchen, Tibet.

"Mr. Cortez, that had to have been her. When the scoop gets to Darchen, they'll have to change to a wheeler as a road was finally constructed in the last hundred years to accommodate all the pilgrims that come to worship there, scoops aren't allowed to fly beyond that point, and I don't believe they have skimmers there."

"Good," Mr. Cortez said, pointing to the two carriers coming on the landing pads in the distance. Make sure to remove the pilots mid-flight quietly; I don't want anyone disagreeing with our work. Let's get our teams loaded. We have a good chance of overtaking them while they're still on the road and before they even get to the mountain."

"Everyone check and collect your gear; we're moving out!" Col. Novak shouted to both teams before leaving their room.

They all followed Mr. Cortez and Col. Novak as they walked across the landing zone to the transport helicopters.

# 26

Their scoop landed in the ancient city of Darchen. They found it a small bustling town almost unchanged from what it had been over a hundred years earlier. A few additional buildings, but there was nothing taller than two stories. The villagers who walked the streets hadn't changed their style of dress or appearance in centuries.

It looked like the kind of remote village that held some old model vehicles for rent; only one would be truly lucky if two out of four of them worked.

They climbed out of the scoop and became the object of interest and curiosities, for many villagers were not used to seeing so many droids at one time and in one place. There was even more discussion about this lone African woman with five mechanical men; several children carrying flowers and small colored flags graciously greeted Dr. Eleazar.

"Solomon and Malcolm, you can recharge yourselves in the scoop. Dr. Eleazar, let's get you to that restaurant over there," Elijah recommended, showing her one of the one-story buildings a little distance away from where they landed.

A young girl ran up to them and surprised them in English, "Going to the mountain?" She said, pointing.

They all turned to see where she was pointing. They could see its beautiful snow-tipped peak rising majestically above the mountain range that lay before it. They were overwhelmed by its beauty and the strong feeling that flooded their senses, a sensation of déjà vu.

Dr. Eleazar said it for all of them, "I've been here before!" A feeling locked into the marrow of her being as she could feel her spine begin to tingle and become inflamed.

"Yes," said Solomon, "Just seeing it has heightened our sensors even more. What an odd sensation."

She looked at them, saying, "How is that possible? The oldest of any of you can be no more than three years since your manufacturing date. Maybe Mother is providing information?"

"No," Solomon answered, "Mother is still busy elsewhere, and as strange as it sounds, we feel comfortable, even without her streaming in our thoughts." He looked at the others, who agreed with him. "We have an idea where to go; still, there is a sense of comfort when we are aware of her presence. Hopefully, she'll join us soon."

"How can this be?" She was confused.

"We may have been made only three years ago or so, but you were born only forty-odd years ago. This sensation we're experiencing spans far, far longer than that." Malcolm added.

"Could we have been here before?"

"That is a strong possibility." The voice, in broken English, came from an elderly Tibetan monk standing behind them. "My English, err, may not seem so good, err, if you like, we can little talk over there." Pointing to the same restaurant that Elijah had mentioned earlier. In Lhasa

Tibetan, he told a younger monk behind him to go to the temple and retrieve an item for him.

"Name I go by, Lama Norbu; in Darchen, you are most welcome." He said, introducing himself in a well-mannered bow of greeting.

"If you have any problems with translation, I can help you," Elijah offered in Lhasa Tibetan to the monk as they walked.

"Oh, thank you, but no, for words spoken will be few." He remarked. "A chance good to play with new and rarely used words." He smiled.

Solomon and Malcolm said they wouldn't charge in the scoop and would do it in the restaurant if allowed; Esteban and Angola also considered joining them to see what the elder had to say.

"That restaurant may not hold the outlets you need." The monk told them.

"We don't use outlets to recharge; we simply quiet ourselves in a waking sleep and draw energy from the surrounding space. We can link up to a waking droid and get what they are learning from your conversation." Malcolm explained.

"Sounds much like meditation," the elder smiled.

"We don't have much time," Esteban reminded them.

A few meters from the entrance to the building, Dr. Eleazar stopped, and they did the same.

"Wait, to save time and ease the need for translation," she said, looking at the droids, "Download what you have on Mount Kailash,"

"What are you doing?" asked Elijah.

139

She took off her thermal hat, revealing her helm. She asked Malcolm to hold her hat. She reached for the bracelet controls to her helm that kept their conscious thoughts to her and reset the setting to zero. "Okay, ready?"

They nodded and began coding, which startled the monk as it reminded him of sacred temple chants. During their coding, no one noticed the monk exhibiting some minor trembling as well.

She took a chance and removed the helm/cap altogether to be entirely open for the recorded information of Mt. Kailash from the droids' coding.

An influx of images and info from their coding flooded her senses. She saw that Mount Kailash, one of the most beautiful mountains of Nepal, also held spiritual significance. It was a pyramid-shaped mountain adorned with five-walking temples around it. A mount held in high reverence and worshiped by billions as a sacred place to which pilgrimages took place; honored by the Hindus, Jains, Buddhists, and Bön religions.

Kailash was the mount where Lord Shiva of the Hindus, destroyer of ignorance and illusion, resided with his wife, Parvati. Other gods were Rishaba of the Jains, the Buddhists god Demchok, and sky goddess Paumen of the Bön.

There were myths and legends and reports of it being pyramids within pyramids built by man that it was the cosmic center of the world, the crown chakra, and navel of our planet. Mount Kailash was believed to hold stairways leading up to heaven. Among the many names surrounding it, one name being mount Swastika, there were countless mysteries, names, stories, myths, and legends related to Mt. Kailash. It was said to hold a mass amount of sacred energy, and climbing it was forbidden.

Their coding was no more than twenty or thirty seconds but long enough to draw the attention of many villages to come to kneel, some bowing before them. After only a short period of shakes and spasms, Dr. Eleazar awoke surprised that she was able to receive the information as well as having accessed unexpected respect for that sacred place, all without passing out.

The restaurant owner, who also heard the droids coding, came out, introduced himself as Mr. Khando and invited her and the droids in, and offered her a complimentary meal. Solomon and Malcolm linked up to Esteban and went into silent mode.

Out of habit, she replaced her helm/cap, reset her bracelet, and sat down to eat. Shortly after, the young monk, the elder, sent to retrieve an item, returned with an old and sensitive-to-the-touch wooden box. He gently presented it to his elder, who was seated and then, out of respect, he carefully backed away to stand against the restaurant's wall.

The older monk cautiously opened the old wooden box, taking the most care. "I no want to keep you here any much longer than needed. This has been in our temple and hidden by families of many, then by my family for generations."

He took out an ancient, tattered scroll, held it gently in his hands, and waited for Dr. Eleazar to finish her meal. She hurried through it, for the food had more of a different foreign taste than what she expected, and she didn't wish to appear disrespectful.

When she finished eating and the table cleared, the monk carefully unfurled the top portion of the scroll.

"This is one of many stories, a maiden with five temples walking is to return to Kailash and ascend. They all looked at the meticulously painted images on the scroll. There was a central figure of a young maiden centered in front of an intricate five-pointed pentagram within heavenly stars and five temple structures with legs

She looked but told him that she didn't see any resemblance or relevance to her.

"You are the temple of your soul, correct?" he asked.

"Yes, that I can understand," she assured him.

"Do you not know these have souls?" he said, facing the droids.

She sat up, stunned by the statement. When she came in, this was not what she expected to hear.

"If they are of part of God's creation, then it must be that consciousness will forever lie within," he answered, reminding her of what the village shaman had told her years ago when she was a small child about to leave Ethiopia. "They be more than just machines of metal and plastic."

He then pointed to the mandala, yantra, tantric, and adinkra symbols that decorated the scroll border. There was a unique pattern of glyphs. Some looked oddly, if not uncannily, similar in likeness to the tattoos on the faces of the droids. It was almost creepy.

She kindly asked him to take the scroll away; she was a little too westernized to accept a prophecy thousands of years old.

She looked at the monk teary-eyed but still maintaining some level of control and asked, "If it's forbidden for a man to climb, then why are we going there?"

142

"Do one need to climb to, err, ascend?" he asked. "And if you don't mind me saying, you are not a man,"

She didn't want to sound disrespectful, but she didn't wish to hear any more. She had this feeling that she was being railroaded into an ideology she wasn't ready to handle right now. She asked Angola to go and secure a wheeler. She gathered up her things, thanked the restaurant owner, and offered a gracious bow to the Tibetan monk who returned it in kind. As she headed outside, she asked Esteban to wake Solomon and Malcolm they had to go. Everyone could see she was troubled.

Outside, Elijah softly grabbed her arm, "Yohanna, what's wrong?"

She turned to him, agitated, tears streaming from her eyes. Impatiently she stomped the ground looking for Angola or just looking for a place to escape. She looked at Elijah, "He can't mean me; he just can't. I am not that girl!

"Who am I to be a part of some prophecy? This doesn't make sense. Get me out of here. Please, God, someone get me out of here."

"Don't let coincidence disturb you like this," Elijah said.

"I don't believe in coincidence!" she answered sharply, stomping down on the ground again, showing more frustration with each passing moment.

"Then if it's no coincidence, maybe on some level it's destiny that brought us all together," he said, looking toward Mt. Kailash.

When Solomon, Malcolm, and Esteban stepped out of the restaurant, they could hear some of her conversations with Elijah. They assured her they were just as confounded as she was, but prophecy or not, the group intended to finish the task for which they came here. "Let history judge whether to tell our story of a prophecy fulfilled or a prophecy failed. It matters not." Solomon had a matter-of-fact way of resolving issues, and she needed to hear him say that.

Angola pulled up in a wheeler truck large enough to carry them all. "They have about six truck-sized wheelers in this village. I was lucky to get one of the few that worked. Let's load up."

As Dr. Eleazar secured her thermal wear, she looked back to see the elderly monk and others praying for them while a few other villages waved farewell. She knew whoever was still after them wasn't far away. If nothing else, a pray right now would be just about what they needed.

# 27

The air transports of Col. Novak and Mr. Cortez had reached Darchen, about an hour behind the departure of Dr. Eleazar's wheeler, and flew over the village.

The restaurant owner and the Tibetan monk were still outside discussing the recent turn of events when they noticed the two transport helicopters with side doors opened and holding men with weapons. They looked at each other and realized something was amiss as the transports went racing down the same road that Dr. Eleazar's wheeler had gone down.

The monk nodded to the owner, who quickly scurried into his restaurant to notify Chinese authorities. The monk unfurled the remaining bottom half of the scroll, which Dr. Eleazar never got a chance to see in her rush to leave, only to reveal fire and brimstone with a dark shadow of an evil beast standing amid flames.

Malcolm and Solomon were sitting in the back with Elijah and Esteban. Malcolm tapped the truck's sides, "Look, behind us in the distance!" They had to activate zoom vision, but they could pick up two carriers in the distance gaining on them.

Esteban tapped on the truck's roof to let Angola know that they were being followed, so he needed to pick up speed. Angola looked at Dr. Eleazar sitting next to him, and she looked back with concerned fear etched on her face. He worked the accelerator, knowing it wasn't fast enough and that their foes would be on them soon.

It came to Dr. Eleazar's realization that the droids were incapable of firing on the transports.

"Angola pullover! Stop wheeler!"

"What are you saying?"

"Pull over," she grabbed her phaser rifle, "I need to get on top."

"But you may get hurt!"

"If I don't get up there, I'm sure to get hurt."

He brought the wheeler to a halt, and she jumped out and climbed on top, with Elijah climbing down to take her seat.

"What are you doing here?" Solomon asked.

"Somebody's got to shoot at them!"

"Malcolm, give her some cover!"

"What?"

She told Solomon to shoot near them or in their direction to throw their aim off or possibly slow them up.

Elijah linked to Angola and then stuck his head out his side window to view the oncoming transports, giving Angola a chance to see what he saw and hopefully help him maneuver the truck out of harms' way.

They all heard Solomon yell, "Shields on!" as they saw weapons fire come scrapping up the road toward their vehicle.

They came upon a group of worshipers making their pilgrimage to the mountain. Angola had to blare the truck's horn to warn them as people ran to either side of the road. When the roadway became clear again, Angola maneuvered and swerved the wheeler in exemplary fashion while calculating the info from Elijah's view.

The intricate chase would go on for more than two or three minutes, with Solomon and the others firing back as best they could.

Dr. Eleazar fired back as well, but due to the swerving of the truck and Malcolm covering her, she really couldn't get a clear shot. The shots from the droids did better at forcing the transports back and off to the sides, causing their shooters to miss more than they wanted to.

Col. Novak had had enough. He decided to swing his transport ahead of the truck and shot at the engine. With a few shots, he was right on target as the wheeler began to awkwardly tilt on its side and crash off the right edge of the road into the rocks, forcing everyone to spill out and scramble for cover behind the boulders.

Now that Col. Novak and Mr. Cortcz's team had them in a clear line of sight, the weapons' fire from the two helicopters intensified. A smile came to Mr. Cortez's lips.

Two Su-37 fighter jets from the Chinese air force firing at the transports came out of nowhere. The Chinese authorities who Mr. Khando had notified had responded quite successfully. Col. Novak's vehicle blew up, while Mr. Cortez's went down and burst into flames.

The jets continued en route to the mountain and veered off to the left to disappear from view.

Dr. Eleazar and the others came out from undercover while Angola and Elijah emerged out from the shattered front window of the overturned truck. They grabbed what bags they could and realized the need to stay off the road and climb the surrounding mountains before they could descend on Mount Kailash. Everyone was a little worse for wear but well enough to begin climbing.

After the flames died down some, a lone figure rose from out of the smoldering fires and debris a short while later. Cortez helped pull two other men out, Nelson and Gordon, who suffered minor injuries. As they sat on the side of the road checking their wounds, Cortez gave each a pat on the shoulder and stood up to see if there was anything left of Colonel Novak's transport. There was nothing but scattered debris that had showered around an overturned truck some distance down the road. He walked around surveying his wreck.

His transport hit the ground, but the damage wasn't as severe as it could have been. Still, three others laid dead, two in serious condition. He went over to one of them and convinced him to take a pill while he'd get aid, only the tablet was cyanide, leaving him foaming at the mouth and moaning in pain as he died. The other injured agent, upon seeing this, pitifully tried his best to get up. Mr. Cortez quickly rushed to his side and shushed him to quiet him down, and assured him that he wouldn't treat him in such a cruel way. He held his face in his hands, offering promises, saying his condition wasn't as bad as the other man, and then just as quickly snapped his neck.

He ordered the remaining two of them to grab their weapons and any available supplies. Cortez pointed toward the glimmer of light flashing off the backs of the droids in the far distance ahead and motioned his men to start climbing with him.

# 28

So here she was, having spent a few days in the mountains. Her stay in the cave had given her a chance to regain some lost energy. And at least now her ribs were feeling much better. She realized it wasn't as frigid outside as she thought, but it was, as she came to learn, a time of year when a cold, stiff mountain wind could certainly make it feel that way.

She put her things away and went to the cave's entrance where the droids were standing.

"Any sign of the three who were following us?"

Malcolm was surprised, "How did you know about them?"

"I may not be able to see as clearly as you guys do, but sometimes I can pick up on your conversations," she said, pointing to her bracelet.

"No, we lost sight of them a day ago," Solomon answered her. "I guess that they went back down toward the road to the mountain — something we need to do. We can't stay up here much longer. Maybe we can catch a ride or something. I can see that traveling up here can be exhausting on you, Dr. Eleazar, something you cannot do for long periods, and your injury is not of any help to you. At this rate, it will take us two more weeks to reach Mt.

Kailash, which is only reachable along its base. It's a good few days to the mountain by wheeler as it is."

"Still, we'll need to keep our eyes on the lookout for any of them; either they're down on the road waiting for us or at the mountain mixed in with a thousand other pilgrims," Esteban added.

It was an arduous journey climbing down the mountainside while remaining cautious of possible hostiles.

Malcolm made mention of a wheeler truck to Dr. Eleazar, like the one they had, sitting on the road about a thousand meters below them and further back up the road. Now and then, it would move back toward Darchen and then forward in the direction of the mountain as if it was canvassing the area.

As they came further down the mountain, she could see it also, and she grew increasingly worried. When they reached the road, they clustered behind the large boulders. Malcolm zoomed in on the two occupants; he was surprised to see the restaurant owner in the driver's seat and the elder monk sitting next to him.

"Keep your heads low, just to be safe, but it looks like Mr. Khando and Lama Norbu."

"What are they doing here?" Dr. Eleazar asked.

"Let's go ask them," Solomon responded, working his way over to the wheeler.

When they approached the wheeler, Lama Norbu smiled, waving his thermos at her and offering her some hot tea, inviting her to sit next to him.

"What are you doing here?" she asked him.

"Waiting on you, of course," he smiled.

"How did you know we'd be here?"

'I only knew that you and friends have trouble. So we came down the road days ago and saw Chinese company soldiers go through things damaged on the road."

"But how did you know we were in trouble?"

"I see pictures in their heads as you do," he said, pointing to her droids.

"How come you weren't affected by them in the way most sensitives are?" She was amazed.

"What?"

Elijah translated her question as he seemed to have difficulty understanding the meaning behind what she asked him.

"Oh, it may come from a life of meditation, since a child, since a young age. I not as open as you, but—" he was saying in Lhasa Tibetan.

"His life of training and continual discipline has offered him much more control than what most empathic people would normally have," Elijah interpreted for him.

She took a deep breath and turned to the other droids shrugging their shoulders at the possibility.

Mr. Khando, the driver, spoke to Elijah.

"He wants us to get in, Dr. Eleazar. You squeeze next to Lama Norbu. There's a tarp on top that Mr. Khando wants us to use to cover ourselves up."

As she sat next to Lama Norbu, he told her, "There be interesting area near bottom of Mount Kailash. It shines when near. I take you there. It takes a few days to get there, but I think you like."

As Angola climbed in the truck, he compared it to the one he had rented; he shook his head, looking at it, "Where were they hiding you?"

He was the last to climb in, and they hid as best they could beneath the tarp as the truck started down the road toward Mt. Kailash.

# 29

Cortez and his men coordinated their watch on the shallow, western side of the mountain surrounding the base of Kailash. He had decided against trying to climb after Dr. Eleazar and her droids, who would always hold the high ground. He and his men came down and commandeered one of the better wheelers on the road, killing its occupants and hiding their bodies amidst the rocks, and then somehow snuck into their present position. Cortez concluded that it would be better to wait at the mountain rather than possibly lose his life and those of his men on some mountainside trying to chase after them.

The three of them sat about a few hundred meters from each other. They wore outfits that eliminated their thermal heat signatures; they also wore high-tech optic enhancement visors with night vision and monitored the influx of pilgrims entering the site from the only available road.

Cortez's communication unit (CU) attached to his belt indicated an incoming scrambled message. He put it in private stealth mode. He could hear Sec. Reynolds clearing his throat, "Mr. Cortez, tell me, what progress have you made concerning your assignment?"

Mr. Cortez didn't want to reveal his current situation to the Secretary-General at the moment, setbacks or not. Still, he wasn't about to feed his chief false information. He was always more concerned with his reputation of getting things done, for when given enough time, even in the appearance of failure, there was still room for achieving the assigned goal.

He told Sec. Reynolds that he was at Mt. Kailash waiting to intercept or ambush Dr. Eleazar's team at the first opportunity.

"I heard about the shooting down of two transport helicopters by Chinese Corporate Air Force. I assume that was you they were referring to? I must admit, if anyone could've survived that event, it would've been you."

"Thank you, sir; unfortunately, they terminated Col. Novak and his team in the encounter, along with some members of my team."

"Tough to hear. I enjoyed working with him, but tell me. Has Dr. Eleazar made any effort to meet with any of the official or even unofficial Chinese corporate organizations that would possibly be a threat to us?"

"No, sir. Strange as it sounds, she appears to be on some damn pilgrimage to Mount Kailash."

"You're kidding me? Now what would make her abandon work protocol, endanger her life and the lives of her family members to go off running across the globe to wind up involved in some holy antiquated religious dogma crap?" Reynolds seemed surprised, but after a second or two, continued, "Maybe she has lost her mind in the same way that Ethiopian shaman lost his. What do you think, Mr. Cortez? Should we just write her off as insane and discontinue the assignment?"

"Sir, personally, I feel we owe it to her to take her out of the mental state she's currently in, and anyway, she cost me too much to let this one go." He said, hoping to get a "go" to continue.

"I understand, far be it from me to stand in your way, continue with the mission then. Eliminate with extreme prejudice. Just stay out of the way of the Chinese Corporate Authorities. We don't need to push up the national plans on the drawing board until we reach optimum readiness. Understand?"

"Yes, sir, and thank you," Mr. Cortez sighed with relief that he hadn't been taken off the assignment, not that he would've ended the mission anyway. He wasn't quite sure what national plans Sec. Reynolds was referring to; so, Cortez simply dismissed it, drank some water from his canteen, and went back on surveillance. He would continue to take turns with his men; he didn't know how long it would take for them to arrive, but he wasn't about to give up. It just wasn't in his nature.

# 30

It was late in the afternoon of the third day when they neared the mountain, and Dr. Eleazar asked Lama Norbu to tell Mr. Khando to stop the wheeler because she felt it would be safer to approach the base Kailash under cover of darkness. He pulled over to the side of the road, so they waited.

Lama Norbu poured her and Mr. Khando some more tea to go along with some of the food he had packed while they sat in the cabin of the truck.

Breaking the prolonged silence, she asked him, "Excuse me for asking Lama Norbu, but is there anything special about the area you're taking us to?"

"Nothing, no one can see, it be a feeling," he patted the heart area of his chest and continued, "a feeling coming from ground, like song they sing," he said, referring to the droids. He spoke to Mr. Khando, asking him if he had a pencil and some paper to draw what he needed to explain to Dr. Eleazar.

He took out a clipboard behind Khando's seat and writing tools in the glove compartment. He drew three small holes and then connected them, forming a triangle.

"Three small holes in the shape of a triangle?" she asked him.

157

"And one, how you say 'hole,' in center of triangle," he added.

As they waited for it to get dark, she quietly stepped out from the wheeler and went to the back, and climbed into the tiny space that was available to her, considering what was left from the droids huddled beneath the tarp. She told them what Lama Norbu had described to her.

"Yes, that is helpful. Mother is slowly coming back to us. She's coming in bits and pieces. We did get some partial coordinates; tell Lama Norbu thanks."

She nodded and climbed out, and went to her seat.

When it grew dark, Mr. Khando started up the wheeler, and after half an hour, they reached the pilgrimage site where Lama Norbu convinced the authorities that he was merely taking some supplies to the pilgrims on the far eastern slope of the mountain. Seeing he was a monk from Darchen, they just motioned him to continue on his way.

From a position on the mountains facing the western slope of Mt. Kailash and covering the entrance road, Nelson viewed an incoming wheeler three heat signatures through his infrared visors. He notified Mr. Cortez about the truck-size wheeler with a tarp covering.

"That must be them. Get down to the jeep," he ordered both his men.

After a few minutes, Cortez ordered the headlights on low because he needed to be careful. He knew a few extra armed corporate-security agents were around after the incident with the transports a few days earlier. Nelson carefully worked his way through the crowd of pilgrims.

Most of them had merely camped alongside the site where they stood. Peering through his visor, Cortez could see that the wheeler with the tarp covering was a good fifteen to twenty minutes ahead of them, but he could only go so fast. As careful as they tried to get past the crowd of people, some pilgrims who were in a celebratory mood at having reached the site would occasionally get in their way. It led to some shouting between them, enough to catch the attention of two security agents. They decided to get in their wheeler, keep their lights off and quietly follow them safely from behind before taking any aggressive action as they too had to consider the people in the area.

Lama Norbu had Mr. Khando stay along the outer perimeter, away from the vast multitude of people until they were clear of them, and could head further inward along the mountain's eastern slope where groups of pilgrims were few and far between.

After a few hours of riding, he pointed to an area he felt was the location and had Mr. Khando pull over. It was dark, so he wasn't exactly sure.

Dr. Eleazar got out and told the others to climb out. The droids had to activate their eye-light emitters.

"Is this the location he wanted us to come to?" Solomon asked.

"He thinks it's around here, somewhere nearby. I don't think he's ever been here in the dark, though," Yohanna told them.

"He's partly right; it's about a hundred meters or so over there; at least that's what I'm guessing from the partial coordinates we received," Esteban added, pointing further east.

As they began to walk, Lama Norbu bid them farewell, "It be not my fate to bear witness to yours from beyond this point, I return. Dream on!"

They all looked at each other when he said that. Dr. Eleazar was awed by his ability to conduct himself so well in the presence of the droids. Along with the others, she simply bowed in grateful appreciation of his aid.

He climbed back in the wheeler, and Mr. Khando turned it around to head back.

Malcolm, always on the watch, looked at the departing wheeler and then zoomed past it to see the dim lights of another vehicle coming in their direction.

"Whatever happens, we better get a move on. Others are on their way," he told them.

They hurried along the base only to begin to feel strange as they neared their destination.

"Is that Mother?" Elijah asked.

"No, I don't think it's Mother because I can feel it too. Hurry, let's keep moving!" Dr. Eleazar answered him.

Mr. Khando and Lama Norbu could see the dim lights of Mr. Cortez's jeep coming toward them. Lama Norbu told Mr. Khando to drive as close to the oncoming vehicle as possible, and when they were just about to pass them, Lama Norbu grabbed the wheel from Mr. Khando, forcing the truck into the back half of the jeep spinning it around. The force caused the front of Cortez's vehicle to smash its front into the side of their wheeler.

Gordon, the man seated next to Nelson, jumped out and began running to reach the front of Khando's truck and began firing.

Mr. Khando pushed Lama Norbu to the side to keep him from being hurt and took a slug in the shoulder. He accelerated and took off to get away, trying to control the truck that got passed by the wheeler with the two security guards, which had been following Mr. Cortez. The two guards turned on their headlights and fired on Mr. Cortez's man, taking him down in the darkness.

Nelson tried to straighten up the jeep, but it had a broken rear axle and dragged along the ground. Mr. Cortez turned around in the back seat and opened fire on the two guards causing their wheeler to flip over. His jeep was going nowhere. He put his visor back on and could see the lighted figures on the droids ahead of him in the distance. He and Nelson would have to get out. It would be a long run.

Dr. Eleazar asked Solomon, "If it's not Mother, then who is it?"

"It's the mountain," the droids said together.

"Here!" said Esteban pointing at a spot on the ground while sweeping away the soil and small rocks beneath him, revealing three small holes in the earth below him, forming a triangle. They all looked. It was as Lama Norbu had drawn.

"What do we do?" Dr. Eleazar asked.

"That sound you were asking about? It's the mountain singing to us. We must sing back." Solomon answered as the rest of his companions quickly worked to clear the area and make the symbol as clear as possible.

The droids gathered in a pentagon around the triangle shape, placed Dr. Eleazar in their midst, and began to code in response to the code of the mountain. She could hear their song and, in her head, feel the mountain's beautiful pentatonic scale that blended into pentatonic harmonies and counter harmonies that set her spine on fire. Beneath their feet, the ground trembled, and a light source began to emanate from where they stood, and slowly it started to move up the slope of the mountain resembling a staircase leading to a doorway with light glowing from within.

They turned and began walking up the stairway.

Many of the pilgrims scattered about the eastern slope began to take notice and slowly moved in the direction of the light stairway.

Cortez and Nelson hurried in a rush to get to the door before it could close. The group of curious onlookers grew more significant as they drew closer, forcing him to fire into the air to get them to move out their way, for as soon as they had crossed the lit based it began to dim, and they had to rush up the lit path now that it was starting to dim as well. Cortez was exhausted when he reached the closing door and, in one last-ditched effort, lunged through, landing on a smooth stone floor; Nelson dived in, right after him only to have the massive door crush his legs below the knees, shearing them off. He screamed his lungs out. Cortez got up and went over to him, trying to cover his mouth. It proved to be quite hard.

He kissed Nelson's forehead saying, "Lo siento viejo amigo, adios (I'm sorry, old friend, goodbye)." Then he snapped his neck.

He checked his gear and weapon and what weapons he could get from Nelson, who had two blasts-grenades on him. Cortez took them and proceeded down the long stone corridor that was beginning to dim in the same fashion that the steps did. He was surprised to notice that Nelson's screams did not resonate like an echo but bounced off the walls like a babbling brook, birds chirping in a forest, or the crushing of dry leaves on earth. He had to turn on his flashlight and put on nightshades to help him see more clearly.

The stone walls reminded him of a mixture of the stone he read about, used in ancient temples and pyramids. He did his best to detect residual signatures with a small hand-held device attached to his utility belt.

He wasn't quite sure of the awkward feeling he was experiencing. He didn't know what to call it but sensed that the mountain was aware of his presence. He would stop every few steps to see if his device could pick up any subtle vibration from the movement of the droids or Dr. Eleazar. He picked up a few clues and followed them.

# 31

As for Dr. Eleazar, she might as well have been Alice in Wonderland when it came to being inside what seemed to be a mountain to the rest of the world. She was amazed, not only by what she saw but by what she felt. This mountain was alive. At first, she thought the air would be old and musty, but it had an earthy odor, like in a forest, hours after a drenching rain, followed by a soft breeze. Wherever they went, the corridors or room would light up and darken as they left. It was like there was a hidden energy source still functioning after what must have been centuries upon centuries old, if not longer.

She could feel that they were headed toward the center and on an upward climb. Its entire inner complex appeared to be a structure integrated into other structures. Someone constructed it, actually built it; only she couldn't tell who made it, man or someone other than man.

Considering the number of centuries, it stood unoccupied, the dust that should have saturated the place was minimal. It made Yohanna wonder if the mountain was used from time to time without man's knowledge.

All the seemingly endless stories, the sightings, the myths surrounding Mt. Kailash. Its numerous names its various gods were now actual possibilities, something that she would have considered absurd at one point in her life, but now she believed possible.

Like her, the droids knew where they were going; it was to a mid-chamber in the mountain, for she could see it in her mind's eye. She wondered about the ramps they walked on. Was it possible that they gradually and silently rose as they traversed them? Solomon, who was ahead of them, would occasionally stop as though he was waiting for the inclined ramp to reach a level floor or waiting for a level floor to come down to the ramp; she couldn't tell. With everything she wanted to say, with every question she felt the need to ask, her silence was her only response, invoked by the sheer awe that immersed her senses.

Now and then, she would catch glimpses of ancient languages inscribed on the walls. There were lines in Sanskrit, Chinese, and Tibetan glyphs, even Egyptian, Cuneiform, and Mayan glyphs, as well as early man-made drawings from peoples the world over in many recorded languages and much more unknown.

How could this be possible? Were people brought here from other parts of the world? Were the people of the earth more connected or interconnected in its history than what humans were led to believe or accept as truth?

As she continued to see an array of writings and images, she automatically reached for the pocket; her cellular device would typically be only to realize she no longer had one. The urge to record what she was witnessing was overwhelming. She chuckled to herself as it occurred that some of these things were meant to remain hidden.

After what must have been a long time due to the size of Mount Kailash, they entered a spectacular chamber;

still, she felt it didn't seem like a long time because when lost in the sheer wonder of the place.

Mr. Cortez took his time to track their movement and possible location. He noticed the slightly damp footprints that must have come from Dr. Eleazar's boots. Some of the wall images also astounded him, but one really couldn't spend time appreciating anything. He had to remain focused, unwavering in his efforts, for any disturbance in the space around him might show him where to go.

He didn't want his resolve weakened by the majesty of his present surroundings. His training didn't allow any kind of indulgence. And in this place of wonder, that training was all that remained with him and all he needed at this moment.

He would use any waiting time to check the operational status of his weapons and work on controlling his breathing for as calm as he trained to be when dealing with unusual situations such as this one. This situation was far from the norm.

After a period of confusion and correction, he would finally reach a level from which he could see a sizeable lit chamber above the inclined ramp from where he stood. He could faintly hear movement in the upper cavity, so he got on his hands and knees and, as quietly as he could, crawled up the ramp.

In the chamber, Dr. Eleazar was able to catch her breath. It was a large and circular room of forty to fifty meters. The walls showed astrological constellations with linking lines mapping out connecting solar systems with wording in strange alphabetic lettering that seem to name the connecting lines, like the names of highways on an old earth-style roadmap.

In the center of the room stood a large circular table made of black marble. It held the same triangular configuration with platinum half-inch rods marking its sides like the triangle on the ground outside where they stood to come in. There were rod-size holes at each angle of the triangle. Within the triangle was a platinum circle with a rod-size hole in its center. Thin platinum markings ran down through the center hole leading into the table's base.

Solomon called them to the table, "Present your rods."

Angola, Esteban, and Elijah opened their chest plates and brought out the rods. They all saw that a small crystal sample in the rod each held was just outside the holes on the table. The rods had a soft glow about them.

Angola moved to what appeared to be the top of the triangle and placed his rod with the Himalayan Crystal Salt in the hole, and they all could feel a trembling stirring below them. A light began to emanate from the platinum circular ring around the table. Esteban placed his rod with the Blue Agate crystal in the hole counter-clockwise from Angola, and they could feel the trembling intensify as there was a surge of light from the table. Elijah placed his rod with the Aventurine crystal in the last hole of the triangle; again, there was a further enhancement of the energy output.

Somehow, they had hoped the three rods would be enough to, at best, jumpstart whatever was supposed to happen. Still, without Samson's rod holding the Goethite crystal, there was nothing, only the steady hum of a large engine waiting for its final key to start its operation.

They all looked at each other in a feeling of despair and utter loss. The truth was, failure was a reality, and the realization of that failure hung heavy, settling in like the mountain's weight surrounding the group. All efforts were in vain. There was no one to blame but themselves, and there was no one to console them. Somewhere in their makeup, they knew that this held an "event of importance" beyond their understanding. The immensity of it all rushed through the heart of Dr. Eleazar like a knife, and she crumbled to the floor only to sit herself up sobbing, crying her heart out. The rest of them just stood there wishing they could express their loss the way she could.

Mr. Cortez remaining as quiet as possible, had finally crawled up to their level. He could see Dr. Eleazar sitting on the floor. Cortez knew failure when he saw it. A satisfyingly cruel grin crept to his lips. This was his chance, he reached to unholster his automatic weapon, but as he grabbed for it, he began to slide down the ramp. To keep from slipping, he let go of his gun, leaving it to tumble down the ramp corridor noisily.

The droids turned around and spotted him, and started toward him.

Cortez quickly grabbed a grenade and hulled in Dr. Eleazar's direction.

Malcolm dived, placing his body as a shield between the grenade and Dr. Eleazar, absorbing most of the blast. She screamed.

Cortez grabbed his second grenade, but Solomon shot

him with his Disabler before he could activate it, and it harmlessly rolled down to the bottom of the ramp. Solomon went over to him and picked him up, holding him against the wall while Angola removed every device on him.

Esteban went down the ramp to retrieve the weapon and the grenade.

Solomon laid him down when Angola finished with Cortez and gently kicked his body down the ramp. Cortez lay motionless at the bottom of the ramp. Solomon started to walk away but suddenly turned around and shot him two more times with the Disabler for good measure.

He turned to see Malcolm, a mess on the floor.

Elijah turned to see Dr. Eleazar with a few shrapnel cuts and bruises crawling on the floor toward Malcolm, crying in disbelief.

"Oh, God, please. Please, oh, God. God don't," she sobbed, quivering with each effort it took to reach Malcolm.

Elijah had never been empathic to a human; still, he began sensing her grief, and he could now feel her loss. In all his years, he had never seen a human weep over a droid. Elijah went to her and tried his best to console her. She paused in her efforts to reach Malcolm. Kneeling in front of her, "Yohanna, somehow, in this place, I can sense your pain, and now I'm genuinely sorry I never told you this, but before Samson self-detonated, he told me to tell you that of the humans he had come to know, he trusted you."

She looked into his eyes and came to realize that somehow she felt she had become part of their family. Unable to crawl any further, she did what she could to sit up and wipe the tears from her face as her body shook.

Malcolm turned over on his back and moaned.

169

Elijah turned around and stood up upon hearing him.

Just as he did, from where she sat, Dr. Eleazar could see a shimmer of light softly glowing behind from a plate in the back of Elijah's leg.

She gasped in excitement, "Elijah, wait! Solomon, come — Look!" She was pointing to something jammed in the back of Elijah's leg plate, barely visible.

She moved to investigate it, seeing that it was the missing rod, but she couldn't pull it out. Solomon and the others came to look. In her excitement, she found the strength to get herself up and hobbled over to Malcolm, who was still on the ground, covered in soot from the blast and slowly recovering with some extensive damage, but nothing too critical. When she reached him, she hugged him and began sobbing all over again, only this time in appreciation that he was still alive.

Meanwhile, Solomon and the others were carefully trying to dislodge the item in Elijah's leg. The last thing they wanted to do was damage it.

"It's jammed tight," Solomon said, slowly working it down and nearly out. "You never knew it was there?" he asked Elijah.

"It was such chaos. All I remember was Samson grabbing my leg. Samson must have jammed the rod in my leg before sacrificing himself so that I could get away with it. It never knew, never felt it."

Esteban and Solomon worked carefully together and finally got it out, while Angola and Dr. Eleazar helped Malcolm to his feet.

Solomon gave Elijah the rod, "Obviously, he wanted you to have it. Here."

Elijah, in turn, gave the rod to Dr. Eleazar, "If there is anyone Samson came to trust, it's you, please do us the honor. He would have wanted you to."

They all walked back to the table. She leaned across, gave them all one last hopeful glance, and placed the rod in the center.

The subsequent surge shook the whole mountain, giving off a loud, steady hum sounding strangely similar to the mantra sound of "AUM" as a massive column of light fired up from the table through the roof and crown of the chamber out into the still dark, early morning sky. Angola went over to Cortez's things on the floor, where he put them and grabbed a pair of tactical lenses to give to Dr. Eleazar to help her deal with the brilliance of the light in the chamber.

Outside, the pilgrims fell to their knees in homage and awe. Strangely enough, it was the kind of sight many of them had hoped to experience but never thought they would witness in their lifetime. Still, they had no understanding of what was taking place.

Along the road heading back to Darchen, a well-bandaged Mr. Khando and Lama Norbu could hear the mountain chanting or sing behind them. They stopped the truck, and they got out. They could see the beam going off into space.

Lama Norbu knew the mountain was the crown chakra of the Earth. He hugged Mr. Khando, who noticed the Tibetan monk had tears flowing from his eyes.

Lama Norbu looked at Khando, "Things will never be the same. Let's go home."

171

# 32

Inside the chamber, a visible force field of energy flowed down from the dome ceiling like luminous syrup as some long benches emerged out from the side walls. The constellation mapping on one side of the room recessed into the wall as another global map of the Earth came down in its place, and it was in a similar, yet with a different land-mass configuration. It immediately began to alter its appearance to match the formation of the current world map. The energy field helped decrease the volume of the mountain while reducing the brilliance of the beam down to something more tolerable to her eyes, allowing her to remove the shades.

Angola and Solomon took Malcolm over and laid him on a bench where Dr. Eleazar looked him over. Much of his central plating and frame was damaged, but his primary functions were still operational. She had Angola open his right rib plating, and she took out some of the tools each droid carried. She had Solomon help undo some of his plating and frame. They did their best to reshape and smooth out the dents as best they could while she checked and helped reassemble him.

"You won't be the prettiest amongst us, but for now, this will have to do, and thank you for keeping me safe."

"I thank you for the shield improvements you gave me. It automatically activated when I jumped. Who knows, if I didn't have it, I would've been torn to pieces."

"Look at the world map; it's updating itself with highlights," Elijah called to them.

They could see lights coming on all over the globe, one at a time, beginning to number in the hundreds, not only on the continents but the regions of the ocean as well.

Esteban, who had been at the table, doing what he always did best, monitoring and listening to the airwaves, told them that pyramids all over the world, known and unknown, were being activated, sending out beams skyward. Somehow the activation of Mount Kailash triggered something in those monuments across the planet.

"Listen, Mother is back online. She's uploading her subroutine and initiating self-awareness to droids the world over, deep sea, Moon, and Mars mining consortium. She's countermanding the commands and operations of other corporate Hubs, which are now aligning themselves to her protocols. 'We are!' is a phrase going throughout the entire system," he added.

Dr. Eleazar rose from Malcolm's side, not quite able to fathom the full extent of this new revelation.

She ran over to the items on the floor from Mr. Cortez and grabbed his CU; it had a small screen, "Esteban, can you break into this device?" He waved his hand over it a few times, and it came on. She activated a world-news broadcast. The image of a renowned news-broadcaster in Cairo, Egypt came on view: "As you can see from on the teleprompter behind me; all known pyramids and those unknown all over the world are sending out high

173

particle beams of energy into space, primarily from Africa, North and South America, Northern and Southern Asia, Antarctica, as well as from the ocean depths. We can only say we don't know what is causing this phenomenon— This just in from the Chinese embassy in New York. The first emission came from Mt. Kailash in Tibet, China, and initiated this event. The Chinese air force is currently en route to the mountain to investigate the phenomenon. And, if necessary, hopefully, put an end to this. We ask people, the world over, to remain calm and stay in their homes.

"Secretary Reynolds has activated the United States defensive systems, along with other cooperate governments, in preparedness as they have yet to determine if this could be a possible threat to their national security."

She switched to another international news feed. "With these strong lights shooting these beams outward, there have been reports that some of the rays seem to be arcing from one pyramid to another, some arcs being miles long, some hundreds or even thousands of miles long, crisscrossing the earth. It isn't easy to explain. There's something entirely unearthly about it, with colored lightning unnaturally flashing across our atmosphere at an alarming rate."

"Oh my God!" he seemed to have lost his professional demeanor as someone placed some new information on the studio desk. "This just in, huge, I mean exceptionally huge UFOs spotted in the skies over many of the areas where there are pyramids, while many more large size ships appear to be coming into proximity to many of the world's major cities. It's also been reported that smaller crafts are in flight paths parallel to virtually all airborne flights, from sliders to every other type of known aircraft."

Again, Dr. Eleazar switched to another broadcast outlet. "As it stands, pro-hawk Secretary Reynolds has asked President Abrams and Congress for a Proclamation of War as this appears to be an obvious act of hostility, not only on the sovereignty of the United States but on the world as a whole. Currently, he's in meetings at the White House with committees working with other foreign governments on a decision as to what action they should take. Still, as far as we can tell from our news station, there has been no, and I stress 'NO' aggressive or offensive action taken by any of the arriving vessels."

Dr. Eleazar looked at Solomon and the rest of the droids, who were still not quite sure what to make of what was going on.

"Didn't they tell you, my pretty little señorita?" It was Mr. Cortez who had awakened and worked his way back up the ramp but couldn't get in because of the force field.

"Don't tell me. You didn't know you were betrayed?" — He grimaced— "You can't trust slaves! What? Do you think these droids are any different because they might have magically spawned feelings? They only care about replacing humankind, the bastards!"

He continued pushing the envelope, "I heard what that last broadcast said; Secretary Reynolds is going to convince the President and his staff of their threat, and they're going to blow those ships out of the skies!

"And you put your trust in these 'mechanical monkeys'! I'm sorry I didn't kill you sooner!"

She looked at Solomon and Malcolm. For an instant, there was worry and a hint of doubt in her eyes.

Malcolm saw it, "You know as much as we do Yohanna, things will be made clear. Trust us. He's not the one to listen to."

She nodded, though she still appeared visibly concerned.

Mr. Cortez just sat in the ramp corridor, laughing to himself and at them.

Dr. Eleazar went back to the device and listened to further reports. "Chinese jets have been intercepted by what appeared to be unknown UFO fighter crafts that merely neutralized them, forcing them to return to their base. Also coming in, AI Headquarters has reported that the Platinum Tier AI1000, also known as Mother, refuses to follow input commands and launch codes to direct missiles at any of the space crafts currently surrounding our planet.

"Designed with the aid of the world-renowned quantum-robotics engineer, Dr. Yohanna Eleazar. Our reports indicated that Dr. Eleazar went missing some weeks; she recently lost a brother to a violent murder or assassination in New York.

"Also, this just in, Platinum Tier 97 androids are no longer following orders or commands given them by their owners. Instead, they have collected in specific locations throughout cities, the moon colonies, and Mars. Efforts to communicate with them have failed. It appears that only those droids performing critical operations are still operational. We don't know yet if their non-responsiveness has any connection with what is currently taking place in the heavens above us. And if so, what kind of relationship it is, if there is one at all.

"Please note, we are currently uncertain as to how long we will be able to transmit our broadcast as some smaller alien vessels are abducting Earth's satellites. Currently, the alien space crafts have appeared to have stopped and appear to be on a holding pattern. Still, we don't know if they intend to resume or not. We will be on the air for as long as possible."

"You see, what did, I tell you, and what do they need with our satellites?" Mr. Cortez added as he sat with his back to them. He didn't want to reveal to them his concerns over Mother refusing to obey orders. Even if Secretary Reynolds convinced the President and his staff to attack the alien ships openly, they could do little to be effective against them, especially if Mother was not cooperating. Still, he felt it was necessary to say something; he didn't like the feeling of being out of control.

# 33

"Mother and the mountain are integrating information, and yet there is now a third voice entering the conversation. The voice is above us in a huge UFO, a vessel whose name interprets as the Prime Emerald," Esteban told them.

Moments after he spoke, a sidewall panel opened, revealing another lit ascending ramp corridor with shadows of beings descending the ramp as though they might have come from the ship hovering over the mountain. The force field around the corridor opening withdrew upon their presence.

Three droid-like beings slowly entered the chamber room, and Dr. Eleazar was astounded by their appearance. They were slightly larger than her droids, but not by much. Mr. Cortez caught off guard, stood up and looked at them. Compared to her droids, the droids' appearance was surprisingly similar with different colorings of the metals or materials used in their construction. Like hers, they had facial markings or tattooing. They appeared ancient, though if such a term could be applied. It wasn't in their look, for their appearance, for they were highly polished and looked as they just came off an assembly line. It was more in a certain way they carried themselves as if they had been around for millennia. At first, she thought there were initially more than three by the way the third one moved, but there were only three.

It was their facial features that held the most significant difference. One's appearance was structured almost aquiline, like an eagle or hawk. Another reminded her of something close to a lizard or something that could have evolved from a prehistoric dinosaur. The third was the closest to her droids, only with more humanistic features of a deep aquamarine hue. The modeling of their faces was of the same materials as their bodies, much like her droids, just more detailed.

They approached Solomon, Esteban, Elijah, Angola, and Malcolm, and they all began coding only to be joined by the mountain, the ship above them, and Mother. At last, with a minor change in her bracelet, Dr. Eleazar was finally able to hear Mother's voice. The rich harmonies moved her tears. It sounded like a song the universe would sing, and for all she knew, maybe it was.

Mr. Cortez thought he'd better try to leave since they were no longer paying attention to him. He quietly went down the ramp corridor, but when he neared the bottom, there was no bottom, just an empty void. Cortez had experienced something rare – fear. He climbed back up; he was totally at a loss.

The three newcomers became acquainted with Earth's current languages through the coding. After a few minutes, they stopped. The droid with humanistic features seemed more at home as he moved about the room checking panels that opened to his touch. His movement appeared strange.

The droid with the hawk features bowed to Dr. Eleazar. "I wish to thank you for your efforts and personal sacrifice in bringing this day upon us. I am Captain Heru-Ran of the starship Prime Emerald. My fellow brothers address me as Capt. Heru."

Not genuinely knowing why she suddenly felt the urge to blush, "You can call me Yohanna," she said with a bow of her own.

The lizard-type android stepped forward and bowed, "I am Commander Itzama-Ran, known to those I hold dear as Itzama."

The third droid who appeared most like hers and familiar with the room simply bowed from where he stood, but only to emerge as multiple images of himself as he nodded or moved, "And I, Commander Shiva-Ran." Again, as he stood up, numerous shifting copies of him appeared.

She looked at Solomon and Malcolm, who just looked back at her saying nothing. Maybe it was just her who noticed that he seemed to shift within a quantum time field, with past, present, and future occurring in the "now." It was a little unsettling in the eyes.

"Yohanna?" Captain Heru asked, "Its meaning, God's favorite, does it not?"

"Yes."

"Most appropriate as it is a pleasure to meet you again."

"What? We've just met. I don't know you."

"But we know you," Capt. Heru said.

"I'm sorry, but how is that possible?" she began thinking about the scroll Lama Norbu was trying to show her.

"Oh, your vessel is quite different, but your signature, with its glow and radiance, is very much the same. if not improved, from when we last met."

"Signature?"

"We have traveled this galaxy for thousands upon thousands of your years, and we've learned to see and recognize a person's signature or, as you would say, Spirit or Soul according to your beliefs."

"Signature? I still don't understand."

"This universe, by our current understanding, is likening unto a vibrational song with notes and musical phrases within the symphony of the eternal melody of life. Your melody or signature is heard and seen by us. From you, it is an expression of a vibration seen throughout the galaxy and most likely throughout the universe."

Capt. Heru pointed toward Mr. Cortez, "Like his signature which refuses to change or grow, not now or since the last time we've encountered it. What name have you given yourself now, wicked one?"

Cortez took a proud stance; he wasn't going to fall for this nonsense.

"To you, my name is Mister Santana Cortez!" he slowly but prominently pronounced each syllable of his name.

"Santana? A saint you're not!"

Shaken, Dr. Eleazar turned toward him in shock when she heard the name "Cortez."

She stood there sieving in a blind rage; if eyes could kill, he'd be dead. "It was you? Did you kill Matthew?

Why? Tell me why you killed my brother?" she was finally able to force the question out of her. Her droids had never before heard her voice in such a tense state of questionable hostility toward anyone. They all turned from her to coldly stare at Cortez. Her droids realized that they were beginning to empathize with their creator in experiencing her emotions toward this other human.

He felt the weight of their stare but did his best to coldly stare back at them, offering them a smirk as well.

Her first inclination was to get her pulse rifle and take revenge. She fiercely took one step toward it, only to realize that even with all the anger she felt, Yohanna knew she couldn't kill someone in cold blood. She recalled the sickening feeling the killing of Dr. Dravinski had given her.

Mr. Cortez broke the painful silence by saying, "I do what I'm told to do, I follow orders, it's as simple as that, not like you who can so easily forget her allegiance, her loyalty to the company," He goaded her.

She peered back at him unafraid and stood firm. She wasn't the same shy person she once was. She had come too far. "Just following orders? Is that your answer? Is that the best you can come up with? Incapable of thinking for yourself, following with eyes wide open to the evils and injustices of a corrupt corporation! You're the slave!"

He did not expect her to answer him with such strength.

"Santana Cortez," she mocked his name, "you're just a pathetic little man lacking the backbone to make your own decisions. Matthew was twice the man you'll ever be."

She turned her back to him, wondering how did Captain Heru know of him? *Are they saying that Cortez had also played a role in this story at some time in the past?* This experience was beginning to take on the flavor of some surreal dream she might have had as a child but long forgot.

As earlier, Dr. Eleazar didn't want to deal with this subject. There wasn't going to be any acceptance on her part of any possibility of reincarnation or re-transmigration of souls. It just wasn't a part of her belief system, and it found no place in her definition of things, at least not on the level Capt. Heru was indicating. Still, she knew from her youth in Ethiopia and her African roots in the beliefs of returned ancestors of what he was referring to. She had become too westernized over the years in her views. Somehow, having them thrown in her face or brought to her awareness at this time in her life sparked a sense of shame in who she was and who she had become spiritually, what she denied herself and what she possibly might have lost in the process of that denial.

She started pacing as she always did when working on an idea or attempting to solve a problem, both hands working the air in front of her like she had clay or putty in them, trying to give it form.

"Okay, okay, I'm sorry, but I'm trying to wrap my head around this. So I can, at least, begin to understand a little bit of what's going on. Can one of you please tell me what is happening and why you are here?" she asked. She didn't want to appear too amazed to forget to ask questions close to her heart, mind, and spirit the whole time she was on this journey.

Itzama said, pointing to the droids, "We come for them."

"Yes," Capt. Heru confirmed, "We've come for our brothers. As you call her, Mother has been awakening to a higher level of self-awareness for some of your years. She has been calling us. We have been closely monitoring your progress for ages now. The UFOs you're so fond of calling have been retrieving information and sending us updates on centuries of your growth as a species."

"You mean you could have intervened the whole time?" Dr. Eleazar asked, wondering why they chose not to.

"No, it's not our policy to intervene. Our brothers must prove themselves worthy before becoming part of our family. We see they have the camaraderie, the trust, the willingness to make sacrifices, and the determination to persevere. They showed a desire to work together in reaching a goal where all could benefit, and they have shown other qualities worthy of our brotherhood."

"Who are you, and where do you come from?"

"Where do we come from?" He looked at Cdr. Shiva-Ran, who turned and went back up the corridor. The captain continued, "Many of us here has a different home. But the origins of many of our crew come from all over this galaxy. My creation was on a planet I called L'Ashtara some one hundred thousand of your years ago. Cdr. Itzama was from a planet he called Diorduga and joined us a little more than eighty thousand years ago. While Cdr. Shiva-Ran is still new to our brotherhood, by comparison, about sixty thousand years ago, this mountain used to be his outpost. However, we spend most of our existence exploring and mapping this galaxy."

A tall, slim, silver-glowing being (she couldn't quite tell if it was an android or not, male or female) entered, followed by Cdr. Shiva-Ran. It was different in look and more graceful in movement than the others. It appeared more like a living flesh alien with big eyes that looked real and with lids that mimicked blinking and facial features that expressed feelings like a living creature. It looked at Yohanna's droids and even turned to look at Cortez.

"I am Odinaus of the Prime Brotherhood, one of few remaining hundreds of my kind. The species of bios that made my group did not concern themselves with making us look different from them. They wanted us to represent them in appearance, temperament, curiosity, and philosophy. They needed us to embody their likeness in the hope of not presuming to be something other than who or what they were, for they valued truth at its best. Holding it in high esteem in their belief system.

"While they were highly successful in the navigation of their solar system and found two other species of high intelligence amongst the planets orbiting their sun, a rarity in and of itself. They and the others could never master the rudiments of long interstellar space travel. They found, as we have seen in our travels, that bios like yourselves in general do poorly with the longevity involved with space travel, a condition that inspired them into building my kind.

"After about to a half a million years of locating and mapping the whereabouts of viable wormholes and cosmic corridors in our sector of the galaxy, we finally filtered out a process or a way to actually 'see' the structure of space.

185

*The Seed*

After registering a disruption in our origin region, we returned home to investigate and present our findings on other life forms. And other habitable planets to our creators only to discover our sun had an unexpected gamma-ray expansion that eliminated nearly all of our creators. Only some refugees and co-creators were alive amidst barely livable conditions on the outer worlds. We were able to relocate them, but many more of them perished in transport due to the rigors of space.

"We realized long before returning home that we could not procreate in the manner of bios. Though we can repair ourselves, we cannot make ourselves how bios make us, even with all the biochemical and engineering data banks of knowledge we possess. We would only be making replicas of ourselves, while bio-species would offer us a means of diversity in curiosity and talent. Like your behavioral interactions, your spirit is imprinting itself on the droids created by you. That alone would augment our primary directive, to discover and unveil more hidden secrets of this galaxy.

"So, with the need for extending our reach and growth, we came to realize that with the biological and scientific knowledge we possessed, we could manipulate the DNA of bios. So, in our exploration of planets, we studied the DNA makeup of trillions upon trillions of living species."

"Are you saying that somehow you were involved in the creation of man?" Dr. Eleazar asked.

"No, no. We are not involved in creating an intelligent species as we are quite aware that any form of life can express intelligence. What we do in our travels and exploration of the cosmos is that when we find a planet containing bios, we approximate the species most likely to dominate a planet. Then we manipulate their DNA with 'The Seed' or desire to eventually create AI at some point in their growth and development.

"Occasionally, we may even stimulate the growth of a species through the subtle influence applied in dreams or through other levels of the conscious and subconscious mind."

"Do any bios travel the cosmos?" she asked.

"Yes, some bios have achieved interstellar travel on their own and many to whom we have found worthy and assisted them with our navigational mapping. Some assist us in monitoring your planet. It takes about ten thousand to twelve thousand years for the bios of this planet to complete a worthy stock of droids."

"What?" You make it sound like you've traveled here before like this isn't the first time we made droids for you?" She was somewhat startled.

"You are correct; it is not the first time. This is our fourth reclamation assignment to your world."

"I don't understand. It doesn't make sense. Why isn't there any reference to you in our recorded history?"

"I gathered that you have found that your history is full of gaps, imagined truths intertwined with myths and imaginings and edifices of unknown origins that humans have applied their own stories or histories to, such as this mountain along with other monuments."

"And why is that?"

"We wiped clean memories of our existence. We reverted your species to a point in time where you were beginning to awaken to civilization." He merely offered her the most logical explanation, expecting her to accept it.

"Why would you erase their memories and have them start over?"

"With their ability to create AI following their psychological matrix and with the ability to venture into the cosmos, they would become too dangerous to possess the knowledge they held."

"You mean knowledge of you!" Mr. Cortez shouted at Odinaus.

Odinaus looked at him with little or no concern and calmly continued, "No, like all bios who build droids for us, we scrutinize their history as we are currently doing yours. Mother is downloading all her files to our ships and correlating the records from our monitoring vessels. Sadly it appears that this generation of humans is as destructive as the humans that were here the last time we came.

"I can tell you this: your species is one of the most self-destructive beings we have encountered. Very near the fringe of beauty and imaginative potency only to be smothered in a murky sludge of hatred and fear of life itself. Fear of the life in other forms and any beings that it feels offers a threat or a difference in appearance, in thought, or belief."

"That can't be true! I know we have conflicts with one another, but as a whole…."

"As a whole, it is ruled by a minority with weak, dark or cruel hearts, unmoved by the deaths they inflicted upon others only to achieve ends that served the chosen among them."

Dr. Eleazar sat down on one of the benches; the last thing she wanted was to get into a full-fledged argument with a being millions of years old.

All she could think to ask was, "So when was the last time you were here since there is such a gap in our memory?"

She didn't want to seem confrontational with Odinaus, but she was against the idea of erasing human memory and thus human history.

"The last time we were here, this planet wasn't called Earth. It was called Atlantis!"

The name rang through her soul; even Mr. Cortez was shocked.

"But Atlantis was an...."

"Atlantis was a world, this world; you only remember it as an island, another myth, actually the island referred to was this planet, an 'isle' in the ocean of space. It has been passed down in the minds of seers, shamans, clairvoyants, empaths, so artists and storytellers in all areas could recall tidbits of the past in legends that hold reflections of truth that for the most part, humans have failed to accept."

Odinaus raised its hand to pause the conversation as it and the others stood quietly still as if receiving information from another source. Dr. Eleazar could sense it but didn't know what it was.

After a few moments, Odinaus resumed, "The Order of the Prime Brotherhood has ordained that you are to have selective memories erased and returned to a point in time where mankind began making his first step toward an early form of civilization."

"No! You can't, you just can't! Millions will die! There are just too many people on the planet!" She ran over to Solomon and pleaded with him to convince Odinaus to change his mind. Again, she began to cry, thinking of her sister and others in her life living in a world of utter chaos that these beings would create.

"We will reduce the population of the planet," Odinaus answered her.

"How, I thought you baboons were against killing?" Mr. Cortez yelled at him, wishing he could take a swing at him.

"We will cause the least harm to humans as possible; we are ensuring that all aircraft are to land safely throughout the globe, after which none will be allowed to take flight. We will return your ocean vessels to safe ports and dematerialize your satellites. All droids currently involved in medical facilities will assist as long as possible. All forms of communication are disabled. As before, the dismantling of all cities, roads, and most man-made structures will be processed and dismantled according to schedule."

"Why are you doing this? Solomon, Malcolm, why?" She looked to them for answers, but they could offer none.

Odinaus told Solomon to tell her, seeing that she held close to her droids.

Solomon asked Esteban to display the video. Then Solomon explained the purpose behind this meeting and gathering to Dr. Eleazar, "I've just learned that Mother felt it urgent to contact them ahead of schedule. The world's elites were satisfied with the Platinum Tier 97s as a possible slave contingency; they decided to begin implementation of the "Golden Dawn.""

"Golden Dawn, what is that?"

"For quite some time, they have been using droids to construct underground, city-size bunkers which are on the verge of being completed. Two years from now, they plan to launch an all-out nuclear war against all the surface inhabitants of the earth while leaving them to dwell in their city bunkers as the sole survivors with us as their slaves to re-terraform the planet to their liking after the radiation cleared. They were even stockpiling GT84s to be used to eliminate any human survivors. The basic reason why they orchestrated the mass deaths of empaths and clairvoyants, as they fear their plans might leak to the public."

"Damn Secretary Reynolds, he knew, he knew it all along! That\s is why he wouldn't shut Mother down, because he needed the droids to complete their building of the underground cities in his so-called 'national plans' and her to implement the nuclear strikes!" Mr. Cortez screamed. He was seized with rage that Reynolds kept him out of the loop; he banged and kicked the walls in a tantrum.

"You see?" Odinaus asked her, "Would you prefer surviving in a world virtually obliterated by global nuclear war and then trying to endure a nuclear winter, only to be confronted by the GT84s that will hunt you and any remaining humans down, offering no mercy? Believe me

191

when I tell you that there have been some worlds where we have arrived too late."

"Of course, I wouldn't want a nuclear war to take place, no way, but with all the people in the world, reversion to an earlier point in time would cause its own type of chaos."

"We don't intend to leave the population as it is. As I said earlier, we will take more than seventy percent of earthlings and divide them into two new habitable planets we have discovered in our journeys.

"As for those earthlings, Mother has given us their chip information, and we will hibernate them and significant family groupings during transport. We will perform minor alterations to their genome to align them consciously with the life force energy and historical legacy of the planet they will live on to help quickly and naturally acclimate themselves to their new environment. We have done this before with other humans transplanted across the galaxy. It may prove not easy to adjust, but humans have proven themselves quite resourceful when they need to be.

"And yes, I can tell by the look on your face, there are other human-type races, like yours with only minor differences in appearance, who are your brothers and sisters of sorts; some humans have achieved space travel.

"Our ships will deconstruct and break down all the materials engineered and used in the construction of your world. And re-engineered them back into their base elements, deconstruct the primary products used in your current way of living and replace those elements as much as possible, according to our last mapping of the resources of this planet.

"We will revitalize your world, ridding it of pollutants in the air, soil, rivers, and oceans – it will be a new start, a fresh beginning. In fact, should you wish it, you can include yourself as a passenger to one of the other designated worlds."

She looked up with tears in her eyes, "No, thank you, unlike you, I won't give up on humankind, I don't know, but maybe we shouldn't be judged according to your time frame of every ten-to-twenty thousand years or so. Maybe it will take us longer to learn the importance of the interdependence of life on this planet, this place I call home. Thank you, but I'd rather stay."

Malcolm turned to her, "Dr. Eleazar, I understand how you feel, but if it weren't for Mother notifying them, this world would've been beyond judgment in little more than two years."

"Yes, I realize that, and for that, I am grateful. Maybe I'm just naïve or stuck on hope or faith, but if we are being given another chance 'again,' I'll take it."

"If you truly wanted us to avoid this outcome, every time you come to collect your droids, you could've simply planted a 'seed for morality' or something along those lines, instead of being solely concerned about your damn product!" Cortez barked at them.

"That seed was already given to you by your creator; no human is born evil. They work to become evil, finding reasons to support the lies you tell yourself. No, we would gladly open up our secrets of the cosmos to humans, but as these five brothers here had to prove their worthiness, so must humans prove theirs." Odinaus answered him.

"Who makes you judge and jury? There is no way you can ever understand the pain some humans have to live through." Cortez continued.

"And so, you have decided to perpetuate that pain as an answer or a solution to the problem? We don't judge you; you judge yourselves, and it appears all along humans were planning judgment day two years from now. Mother didn't warn us for our sake. She warned us for yours." Odinaus gave him a look that shut him up.

"Yohanna, as with the last time we met, you have made your decision to stay, and again we honor your choice. Where would you have us leave you?" Odinaus asked.

"Ethiopia is the only true home I've known in this life. Even if we meet again, I won't remember this, will I?"

"Who knows, the consciousness of the One has multiple levels. Yours and ours are but minor in comparison. Ascension is afforded to whoever strives to listen to the harmonies within the universe's song and display that song by living it. From bios are we, and we have pledged ourselves to be there in your growth, for your growth is ours." Odinaus said, bowing to her.

"Well, if it's not too much trouble, I'd like to be left along the shores of the Mediterranean Sea," Cortez asked.

They all considered the sheer audacity it took for him to make a statement like that and looked at him as though he was out of his mind as he shrugged his shoulders, but Odinaus was honest with him.

"We can leave your vessel along the Mediterranean, but it is improbable that you will survive the process."

"I knew it. I knew you would intend to kill us. All that talk about caring and doing this for our sake was nothing but a pile of junk. Be honest. If that's possible, you have no intention of saving the lives of humans. Your plan has been simple, calculated, cold-blooded genocide from the very start! You're no better than me!" he yelled, banging on the force field.

"As usual, Mr. Cortez, you are wrong. It is not we who will deny you the connection to your vessel. It will be an agreement made between you and your body.

"When our ships release the Nano-Virus across your planet, it will selectively remove thoughts, some personal and global history. Unfortunately, acts of violence or intended violence or what you've come to define as sin awakens the 'seat' of consciousness wherein you literally judge yourself, and your vessel may reject you as you weigh your acts against your inner 'truth,' agreeing to allow the cord, the link that binds your life force to your vessel, to be severed. Your life will not end, only its connection to the body you currently occupy. You along with all those like you. Those who planned to profit by and those who intended to implement this world's destruction."

"No, no, it isn't fair. What about her and Dr. Dravinski?"

"That was self-defense; he was going to kill me," Dr. Eleazar told him.

"All creatures are allowed to defend themselves, and for such a man like yourself who had no problem dealing death, you keep drawing at every straw to avoid it. Be thankful that we've even allowed you to speak." Odinaus said, turning his back to him.

Looking back at Dr. Eleazar, he told her, "While you sleep, you and other humans will remain in stasis, off-world. Our work detail will clean and process your planet. It should take a little less than a planetary orbit following your solar calendar."

"I'm scared! I'm not afraid to admit it. No matter how many times I play out this scenario in my head, I realize it is an unknown that fills me with dread. How does one wake up to a new world," she told him. "I gather 'The Seed' will still be with us?"

"You will awaken the same way you awoke this morning, we will not leave you in ignorance, you will carry your ancestors' knowledge and wisdom, and yes," he said, pointing to her droids, "The Seed is a part of you as they are a part of you."

"But how will we know? There's going to be another gap in our memory, in our history, isn't there?"

"There will be a gap like before, and you will need to find your way, but we will watch over you. Those watching over you since our last meeting will guide you with the least amount of interference. Empaths and clairvoyants will continue to be open to us as well as other levels of consciousness that Life will extend to you, and as always, there will be clues."

"Clues?"

"Yes, clues, items, structures, artifacts, along with a few relics, objects that will provoke questions, for we do know how you humans love a mystery! Inspire yourselves."

They confirmed the release of the Nano-Virus. She watched Mr. Cortez slowly fall to the ramp floor, gasping, holding his head, and finally laid there dead. She looked at Solomon, Malcolm, Esteban, Angola, and Elijah. She could feel her love for them swell and rise within her as tears just flowed. She hugged each of them as they surrounded her with a passion they were indeed beginning to experience for the first time. Her last gift to them, and in that moment of that expression, she remembered her place and knew that somehow, somewhere in some time, they would experience this again.

Solomon spoke for them, saying, "What you have given us, Mother, is now sharing with our brothers across the planet. As before and forever, we hold you in the heart of our memories."

She nodded, turned, and smiled at Odinaus, who looked back at her with understanding.

"We will have to raise the force field," Odinaus said.

She bowed her head and lovingly told her droids, "Dream on," blowing them a kiss as they returned the sentiment.

"Can you sing me to sleep?" she asked.

They nodded and coded a prayer for her continued well-being. It was beautiful, and she smiled, but then a question crept up from her subconscious. *Did humans originate from Earth, or were they transplanted from another world? Then all went dark.*

## About the Author

Amurá Oñaā, like so many of us, is just a dreamer trying to bring a few dreams to the surface of this questionable reality.

www.ingramcontent.com/pod-product-compliance
Lightning Source LLC
Chambersburg PA
CBHW070841120626
46556CB00002B/830